Traded for
One Hundred Acres

Traded for
One Hundred Acres

Karen Ayers

Strategic Book Publishing and Rights Co.

Strategic Book Publishing & Rights Co., LLC
USA | Singapore
www.sbpra.net

For information about special discounts for bulk purchases, please contact Strategic Book Publishing and Rights Co., Special Sales at bookorder@sbpra.net.

ISBN: 978-1-950015-86-3

To Jim, my husband, for loving me. Thank you for making me feel special and for writing the poetry for this book. I love you, sweetheart!

****

To Ken, my investor and friend. Thank for believing in me and encouraging me with my writing. You believed in my writing way before anyone else did.

****

To Angela, my daughter. I hope you know I smile each time I think about how much you love our Lord. You have had a hard life from time to time, but you have the most amazing forgiving heart. I am so glad I made you my daughter.

****

To Jennifer, my daughter. I will never forget the night you looked up at me with those tiny eyes on that cold winter's night in January. I had no idea how to be a mother, and I had to learn it all with you. I treasure the bond you and I share and pray that you and your own daughter will always be as close. You are a terrific mom and hairstylist, and I am so proud of you.

****

To Kris, my son. You came into my life at such a young age and called me Mom. Even though I am no longer married to your father, you are no less my son. I loved you then, and I still love you now. Follow your heart, son, for there isn't anything you can't do if you put your heart in it.

****

To Mary, my daughter. I love you, Mary, and think about you often. If you ever read this, please email me. I will never regret adopting you and would love to be a part of your life.

****

To Heather, my daughter, my sweet baby girl. I have watched you grow into such a well- educated, independent young woman who is beautiful inside and out. I am so proud of the woman you have become and know you are a great teacher that children look up to. Looking forward to seeing what the future holds for you. I have no doubts it will be amazing.

****

To Lance, my son, the youngest of the clan. Thank you for being one of my best friends and being a boy who is such a delight to raise. Thank you for doing much of the research for this book; you are so bright. I pray that life gives you all that you hope for. Never let anything keep you from going after your dreams.

****

To my children by marriage, Megan, Whitney, Brandon and Jordan. I hate the word STEP-children. So, I will just call you children by marriage, if you don't mind. I want you to know I love each of you, *and I am so glad you are now in my life. Even though I will never take your mother's place, please know I am here should you ever need me.*

****

And thanks to all my fans and friends I haven't mentioned by name. Just because your name isn't here doesn't mean I care for you any less. I have met so many wonderful people along the way with my books and have no idea what I would do without you reading and promoting. Thanks also for all the kind words you have said to me.

*****

Thanks to Strategic Book Publishing for all the work and effort you put in to make my books look their best. You have such a professional staff that is a delight to work with.

*****

I also want to give a HUGE thanks to the photographer that allowed me to use one of her photos for the cover of this book. Dani Lee Photography of Brooklet, Georgia, I am truly grateful to you. When I ran across this photo, I just knew this was Savannah and Jonah, for the people here are exactly what I envisioned them to be. You can find Dani Lee/Photography on Facebook. She is awesome and very professional.

And let's also give credit to the couple that appears on the cover; Brooke and Aaron. There is a true love story here, for Brooke is a friend of mine and Aaron is her fiancé. They have been sweethearts ever since they were young kids as neighbors and this photo clearly shows their love. Thank you so much for allowing your photo to be the cover of this book.

*****

But most of all I thank Jesus Christ for wrapping me in His loving arms and loving me even when I didn't deserve to be loved. You saved my soul and forgave me by Your grace and mercy. To You I owe EVERYTHING and because of You, I have hope and a future. And because of You, I learned to forgive.

CHAPTER 1

1832 America

****

Alice Bowen listened carefully to the conversation taking place on her front porch. She knew it wasn't polite to eavesdrop on her husband and Mr. Bell, but the things she was hearing were more than her heart could bear.

Mr. Bell had been their neighbor for several years, and today was the first day he had ever visited.

Before today, they only ran into him in town from time to time, but never had he so much as stepped on their front porch, until now, after his wife's recent passing during childbirth.

"There's a right smart bit of land I own, Mr. Bowen, and I am sure, with it already adjoining yours, you have thought of the possibility from time to time?"

Mitchell smiled and rubbed his hand across the three-day stubble on his face. "That I have indeed, Mr. Bell. In fact, I'm willing to meet your price and conditions. When do you expect such a transaction to take place?"

"Pardon me, sir, for giving such short notice, but I would like to get started in order to make it in time to build a cabin before winter sets in. Traveling by wagon in cold conditions is not something I wish to endure. If we embark on our journey in the next couple of days, sir, we should make it there by the middle of summer, which will give me ample time to erect a small cabin before the harsh winds set in from the north."

"I see, and short notice it is, Mr. Bell. But have no fear; I will have Savannah ready to go day after tomorrow. Let me say one thing, if I might. If ever I hear of you mistreating my daughter in any way, I will personally hunt you down like a bear and tear you to shreds." Mitchell smiled slowly and leaned back in his chair.

He liked Jonah Bell, and it was true about him wanting his land, although he had never dreamed of owning it without so much as one single penny being exchanged between them.

It was an offer Mitchell could not refuse. Besides, where else would his daughter find a beau like Jonah Bell?

"I'm an honorable man, Mr. Bowen," Jonah shifted from one foot to the other. "The only reason I asked to marry your daughter in the first place, sir, is because it wouldn't be proper to take her across the land alone and not be married. Truth is, sir, I have no intention of ever consummating the marriage when my heart still belongs to Clara."

Mitchell Bowen laughed, wickedly. "Oh, I suppose that prediction won't last long lying by a girl as sweet as my Savannah. She'll be ye wife, Mr. Bell, and a wife does have her duties to perform for her husband. What I meant was not to harm her. I'm only allowing this because she's already sixteen, and you're the only beau around that's single for hundreds of miles. It's high time I push her outta the nest, so I'll have one less mouth to feed."

Alice gasped and placed her hand over her mouth as she ducked out of sight of the open window.

How could she ever tell her eldest daughter she'd been traded in exchange for land?

How could Mitchell have done such a ghastly thing as this?

It was true what he said about Mr. Bell being the only available bachelor within miles, but that was only because his wife Clara was no longer alive, and it had only been three weeks at that.

It never crossed her mind that Jonah would ask for her daughter's hand in marriage just three short weeks after his beloved wife passed. But, of course, she should have figured that Savannah would be his choice if he was faced with the dilemma of having to find someone suitable to tend his infant daughter.

And why wouldn't Savannah, of all people, be perfect for the job? She'd been helping take care of two younger siblings since they were born. If anyone knew about babies, it was Savannah.

"Alice, come here!" Mitchell screamed out from the front porch. Alice jumped and grabbed at her chest, knowing this day would prove to be the most dreadful day ever. Jonah Bell was headed back down the driveway with his horse and wagon as she walked out on the porch.

"Would you like some fresh cold lemonade?" Alice asked, shaken. The last thing she wanted was to tell her husband she knew of his plans.

It wasn't proper for a wife to listen to her husband's conversations without permission, and if there was one thing Alice knew, it was how to be a proper wife. She had raised Savannah the same way.

"No, I'm not thirsty. I need you to prepare Savannah to be wed to Jonah Bell. She will be leaving with him to head west the day after tomorrow."

Alice looked at Mitchell with a blank stare for a moment. "The day after tomorrow? Oh, Mitchell, what have you done?"

"Nothing that wasn't fittin'. Mr. Bell has a three-week-old baby girl and is headin' west. He planned to go with his late wife, but his plans have been extinguished. He's asked for Savannah's hand in marriage in exchange for his land," Mitchell smiled. "He must have one hundred acres."

"But why would he want to marry again so soon, Mitchell? Why, poor Clara's body isn't even cold. What will people think?"

"Didn't you hear what I said, woman? He has a three-week-old baby and doesn't know a thing about babies. Besides, he will be leading the team. His daughter wouldn't have made it this far if he hadn't hired a wet nurse, and why should ye worry about what people think? No one has cared about our business thus far."

Alice looked out the long driveway and watched Mr. Bell disappear from their sight. "Oh, Mitchell, how can I ever break this news to our daughter? It is simply dreadful. We shall never see her again."

"Every bird leaves its mother's nest sooner or later. Let her go, Alice; she is sixteen and old enough to get married and embark on her own."

Alice reached up and wiped at a stray tear; her heart was breaking. "She's my baby, Mitchell. I shall not bear it. I shall never be the same again."

"Goodness, woman, did you think Savannah would be with us forever? That is not the way it works, and you know it. Besides, Mr. Bell seems like a fine man and you should be happy he has asked for her. I don't see any other beaus knocking on our door, and we certainly don't wish for her to be an old maid."

"He must be at least thirty, not but a few years younger than you and I. Savannah doesn't even know him other than carrying food back and forth from time to time. She has only seen him in the fields from afar."

"Then she will proceed to know him much better," he laughed.

It angered Alice the way her husband joked about something as serious as this. She had never said a cross word to her husband in all their eighteen years of marriage, and she knew it wouldn't be proper to start now. Besides, what would it accomplish to go against his wishes? After all, he was the head of their household, and what he said she would have to abide by, even if it went against her heart.

"But how, Mitchell, how shall I tell her?"

"You shall tell her the truth."

"That her father traded her for one hundred acres?"

Mitchell gruffly got up from his chair and placed his straw hat on his balding head. "Say whatever you wish, Alice, but do as I command."

Alice stood in horror as she watched Mitchell leave the porch and head to the barn. Savannah would be home from the mercantile shortly and would have no idea that she only had one more day in their little town in the northeast Georgia mountains.

It broke Alice's heart knowing how much Savannah loved living in Dahlonega. She was born there and had lived there all of her life.

Their little town had recently obtained a courthouse that stood in the middle of the town square and there was talk everywhere about the first major gold rush taking place now. People were coming from all over in hopes to find gold, and it had just recently changed from being called Talonega, to Dahlonega.

So much was going on in their town, and now Mitchell was having her daughter carted off to the Wild West. Alice feared the Indians, even though so much had settled down with the white men and the redskins, there were still tribes here and there that didn't like anyone trying to take the land they felt rightfully belonged to them. Why, what if she was scalped along the way? All that beautiful dark hair would be a trophy piece to the redskins.

Mary cried out in the back room and brought Alice's attention back to reality. It was past time for her feeding, and Alice knew she must be wet, also.

What a terrible mother she was, so consumed in the things going on that she neglected the one thing that depended on her, her eighteen-month-old daughter.

"I'm coming, Mary," Alice took off inside the house and tried to forget what was to come, if only for a moment.

*****

Savannah loved the way the sunlight danced off the water at Mill's Pond. She wished a thousand times she had more time to come down to the pond's grassy banks and just lie there and daydream, if nothing else. It wasn't easy being the oldest; there was never any time to herself.

She would so love to have more time to write in her journal and write more poetry. Putting words together was something she loved; to describe the way she felt on paper was magical.

She kicked at a rock and tried to pick up her pace. Her mother had sent her three miles to the mercantile to trade their eggs for flour to make bread, and she was certain that by now she should have already made it home.

Savannah ducked behind a large oak and out of sight when she spotted Jonah Bell on the ridge, driving his horse and wagon. There was something about him that made a woman look twice.

Once, at the mercantile, she had gotten close enough to smell the very scent of him, a clean fresh scent that was pleasant, not the way she would have thought a man should smell after plowing the fields all day. The very sight of him took her breath away.

She felt sorry for Mr. Bell, knowing his sweet wife had passed, giving birth to their daughter so recently.

He was the talk of the town, as everyone had their own opinion of what he should do. Savannah wondered how he was caring for such a tiny daughter and doing all a man needed to do at the same time.

She had only seen Jonah a few times but knew he was a man any available woman would love to call her own, and she wondered if he would ever want to get married again. Surely, a few of the ladies in town would gladly say yes to such a fine man as Mr. Bell.

Savannah laughed out loud at the thought. Why was she wasting her time daydreaming? Even though she was sixteen and well on her way to being a proper lady, thinking thoughts about a much older, widowed man was not proper at all.

Savannah took her journal out of her skirt pocket and sat down beside the tree. She was already late; surely a few more minutes wouldn't make that much difference.

I hide behind this big oak tree,
For me, I didn't want him to see.
He is strong and kind,
Thank God for me, he is blind.
I feel foolish all alone.
I wish my heart didn't have to bear,
To admire a man whose heart won't care.
For somewhere else I'll need to find love,
A God I cry to so far above.
Can He hear me or even care?
Will He leave me with this cross to bear?

*****

Jonah let out a huge sigh and shook his head, thinking about what had transpired between himself and Mitchell Bowen.

What would Clara think of him if she knew he had traded all their land for such a young girl as Savannah Bowen, and to be his wife at that?

It had never once crossed his mind in the three short years they were married that he would ever so much as consider taking another woman as his wife.

His plan was to grow old with Clara and watch their children grow up on the land they chose out west. It was *both* their dreams. Something they spoke of each night before bedtime.

Hopefully, she would be proud that he still intended to live out their dream, even if she wouldn't be at his side. He'd made the decision just three days ago and decided to see it through, leaving everything behind but his daughter, a few clothes, enough tools to build a cabin, and someone to care for his Rose along the way.

Savannah was the only obvious choice since she was old enough to care for a baby, and yet single. There was no way he could have asked a married woman to help him with such a feat, and so Jonah had done the only thing he could, to ask Mitchell Bowen to let him wed his young daughter in exchange for his land, the land that he and Clara had planned to sell in hopes to obtain enough money to see them on their journey.

There were only a couple of times he'd laid eyes on Savannah, but from what he'd seen briefly, she was very beautiful and looked much older than her age.

Of course, it didn't really matter what she looked like, since she would never be more than a caregiver to his daughter.

"Whoa," Jonah yelled out, pulling the reins back tight, stopping the wagon in front of the Bakers' small home. Nelly Baker had agreed to keep Rose for him while he set out to talk to Mr. Bowen this morning. Nelly was good to help him since Clara passed, but unfortunately, she belonged to someone else and already had three children of her own.

"You back so soon?" Nelly said, coming out the door, wiping her hands on her white apron.

"Seems like I have been gone an eternity."

"Not long at all. I just told Elijah and the children to wash up for dinner. You're just in time. It's nothing fancy, but I guess beans and cornbread will be okay, eh?"

"Sounds right tasty." Jonah jumped off the wagon and headed for the house. "How's Rose?"

"She seems to have a tummy ache. I guess my milk isn't agreeing with her, but then I'm not her mother." As soon as Nelly said it, she regretted it. "I'm sorry, Jonah. I should watch my words."

"It's all right. I appreciate you taking such good care of her, Nelly."

"Jonah, me and Elijah were talking, and if you like, we would keep Rose for you a while and tend to her needs. That way you wouldn't have to drag her back and forth for me to feed. Or perhaps you'd like to bunk here a bit until she gets stronger and more able to eat with a wooden spoon."

"I do so appreciate that, Nelly, but I will be heading west in two days, and I plan to take my daughter with me."

Nelly looked horrified. "Jonah, you can't lug a baby out west. Whatever will she eat?"

"Been studying up on that, Nelly. She will drink goat's milk. I plan to buy a goat tomorrow."

"Jonah, most babies don't live if they aren't on breast milk. How do you think she will survive on goat's milk?"

"By feeding her with a spoon, of course."

"A wooden spoon? Jonah, surely you have not thought this through. Do you realize how often you will have to feed her that way for her to get the nourishment she needs? How will you guide the horses and feed her at the same time?"

"And I have thought that through also, Nelly. Don't worry none; I have this all figured out."

Nelly shook her head with a look of disappointment on her face. Jonah had been a friend to her and Elijah for years, and she couldn't bear the thought of him taking Rose and heading west. She never voiced it, but he did not like to hold her, and Nelly was almost certain she knew why.

Jonah opened the door and brushed by her. "Just wait until I tell you my plan before you get upset."

*****

"Mother, you have not been yourself this past hour. Whatever is wrong?"

Alice was glad Mitchell had decided to go into town. Telling Savannah had to be done delicately. For the past hour, she had paced so much on her kitchen floor that she was sure she would wear out the planks.

"Come sit down a spell, Savannah. I have something I wish to speak to you about."

Savannah took a seat on a straw bottom chair and looked frantically at her mother.

"Whatever is wrong, Mother? Is something wrong with Father?"

Alice sighed and sat down beside her, glad Mary and Joseph were sleeping. "I have searched my heart for the right words, Savannah, but I am dreadfully afraid that any words I shall choose will not be adequate."

Savannah took her mother's hand and felt her trembling. "Oh Mother, please do tell me what's on your heart."

"Savannah, I am afraid your father has promised your hand in marriage to Mr. Bell."

Savannah froze for a moment and stared into her mother's eyes. She could feel her heart pounding in her chest. Surely, she had not just heard what she thought she heard.

"Promised? Mother, I am confused."

"Your father told Mr. Bell that you would marry him."

"You mean Mr. Bell asked if I would become his wife?" Savannah couldn't believe what she was hearing.

"Yes, Mr. Bell came over to talk to your father when you were at the mercantile. He wants to move out west and wants you to travel with him and take care of his infant daughter."

"Mother, this is preposterous!" Savannah abruptly stood to her feet and flung her arms in the air. "I have no milk, mother; the baby will die. Nelly is taking care of her. She has milk from having her own son."

"Savannah, many mothers die during childbirth. You will feed her with a spoon just as you have your sister and brother."

"But not until they were older. Oh mother, what if I can't care for the child well enough?"

Alice couldn't believe what her daughter was saying. She seemed to be okay with the fact that she would become Jonah's wife but scared to take on such a responsibility as his infant daughter. "Sit back down, Savannah, your father could walk in and this is not a proper tone to be speaking in."

Savannah sat back upon the stool and closed her eyes. "Jonah Bell asked Father if I would marry him. Why, Mother? Why would he choose me?"

"Because you are single and there aren't any single women in these parts. Don't worry, I overheard him telling your father he still loved his wife and only wanted to marry you so it would look good to others. I think Jonah was only thinking of someone to be his daughter's caregiver."

Savannah sighed. "Just as I thought. Mr. Bell doesn't want a wife at all."

"Why do you look so sorrowful? I thought upon hearing that, it would make things easier for you to bear."

"Mother, every girl wants to get married and have children of her own, but Mr. Bell still loves his wife and will never think of me in that way."

Alice smiled, realizing her daughter's heart. "Oh Savannah, love takes time. It is not a hasty thing. Give it time and see what happens. You are a very beautiful, kind-hearted woman, and I am sure, in time, Mr. Bell will grow fond of you."

"I saw him today, Mother."

"You mean Mr. Bell?"

"Yes, going toward his house when I was down at Mill's Pond. He didn't see me, of course, for I hid behind the huge oak there."

"You were spying on Mr. Bell?"

"I was," Savannah smiled.

"Savannah Bowen, just what were you thinking?"

"That he would make any available woman a grand husband. He seems like such a kind, gentle man, and I might say that he is very nice to look at."

"Savannah, I cannot believe you were thinking such thoughts about a man that just lost his wife and is still grieving over her."

"I'm sorry, mother, but I could not help it."

Alice giggled and took her daughter's hand again. "Are you not terribly upset with your father?"

"I do so wish he asked me, but I would have said yes, even then."

"Oh Savannah, that is so good to know. I am feeling so much better now. There is something I haven't told you."

"What, Mother? Please do tell me all."

"Mr. Bell wants to leave the morning after tomorrow."

"Oh Mother, shall I ever see you again?"

Alice stood to her feet and pulled Savannah up, embracing her gently. "Savannah, I have no idea. When one gets married, their entire life changes. I shall think of you every day of my life, and I know that you shall in return think of us. We can write letters to one another. Please don't be sad, for I don't think I can bear it."

"Please pray for me every day, as I shall pray for you. Pray that God will give his infant daughter strength, and she will grow to be a healthy child."

"She will be your child too, Savannah."

"Oh Mother, I had not thought of that. If I marry Mr. Bell, his daughter will be my daughter. I shall be a mother."

Alice smiled. "And you will be a great mother. Just wait, you'll see."

"If that is to be, then it is only because I was raised by a great mother."

"Thank you, and I do hope you are not terribly upset with your father. I do believe he thinks Mr. Bell is a great catch, as well."

"I am not upset, Mother, just frightened and nervous."

Alice turned and picked up her tattered Bible and placed it in Savannah's hands. "Here, take this with you. Read a chapter or two each day and it will help you. God's promises will remind you that you are never alone."

"You have read me many passages from here since I was born, and so it will also remind me of you." Savannah's eyes grew wet.

"Please don't cry, Savannah, or you shall have your mother crying as well."

"I shall treasure this, Mother, all the days of my life."

CHAPTER 2

"Are you ready?" Alice asked Savannah sadly, just before daybreak.

"I am. I will miss you, Mother, and I shall write to you as soon as we get out west, so you will know my address. I shall keep a journal of our journey."

"It will be two months before I hear from you. I prayed last night and placed you into God's hands. He will go with you as He always has."

*****

Savannah willed herself not to cry. The night had passed too quickly without sleep, thinking about the new life ahead of her and what God wanted for her life. Surely, this was His plan, for her to be Mr. Bell's wife and take care of his infant daughter.

"I would love to say goodbye to Joseph and Mary but don't want to awaken them. Please give them a kiss for me."

Alice embraced her daughter tightly and wiped at the tears that were beginning to fall. "I so hoped you would marry a man that lived close, so we could keep in touch, but I feel at peace now. This is the way it should be. I have prayed hard seeking peace over this."

"Yes, Mother, I feel the same. Mr. Bell is a good man, and I am lucky that he chose me. I only hope he never regrets his decision."

Alice pulled away and looked at her daughter once more. "How could he ever regret choosing you? You have been the sunshine in my life for sixteen years, and I know he shall feel the same, given time to get to know you. If you ever get lonely for home and need me, just hold my Bible closely and always know that my thoughts and prayers are with you."

"I shall, Mother. I shall never forget all that you taught me. I would like to say goodbye to Father. Do you think I should wake him?"

"I'm not sleeping," Mitchell said, pushing the curtain aside that separated his and Alice's bed from the rest of the house.

"Mr. Bell will be here soon, Father, and I wanted to tell you goodbye."

Mitchell walked over to his daughter and hugged her tightly. "I hope you have no ill feelings toward me for what I have done. I feel in my heart this is the best thing for you.

Jonah Bell is a good man, and he will take great care of you, I am sure."

"No Father, I am not ill with you. I feel it is God's plan for my life."

"You are not ill that Jonah traded me one hundred acres for your hand in marriage?"

"Mitchell," Alice said, more sternly than she knew she should have. She had not told Savannah about the land, because she wasn't sure how she would feel about it.

"Mr. Bell gave you his land?" Savannah asked, confused.

"Please know that is not the only reason I promised him your hand. The main reason was because you are sixteen and won't get many chances to wed with no available beaus in these parts."

Savannah looked at her mother, wondering why she was not told but knowing there was no time now.

Perhaps her mother wanted to spare her the truth. "I understand, Father. Please know that I love you both, and that I am not ill with either of you."

The sound of a wagon approaching brought their attention back to the task at hand. Savannah was leaving, and Alice felt certain she would never again see her daughter this side of heaven.

"He is here," Alice said, softly.

"Yes, he is," Mitchell agreed, opening the door and looking out at the sky that was now streaked with orange and yellows as the day overtook the darkness.

Savannah started for the door with her bag in her hand and took one last look at her mother and the small home she had grown up in. "I shall never stop thinking about you or what you instilled in me."

Jonah walked up on the small porch and shook Mitchell's hand. "Good morning, Mr. Bowen. Is Savannah ready?"

"I am," she said, coming out the door to face him for the first time.

"I told you she would be, Mr. Bell. I never go back on my word."

Jonah handed Mitchell a folded piece of paper. "And neither do I, sir. I made out a deed to my land. All one hundred acres of it now belongs to you. I left most of my personal belongings, as it would have been too hard to carry across the land by wagon. Do with it as you will."

"Take care of my daughter, Mr. Bell," Alice spoke softly.

"Yes ma'am," Jonah nodded as he took off his hat. "I plan to stop as soon as I find a church and have the parson marry us."

"That is good," said Mitchell. "That is the proper thing to do."

"Where is your daughter?" Alice asked, looking toward the covered wagon.

"She is sleeping inside. I bought a goat to take with us, so she will have milk to drink."

The goat made a noise as if she knew she was being talked about and made Alice smile.

"I see that. Well, don't worry, Savannah knows all about taking care of babies, don't you, Savannah?"

"Yes, Mother," Savannah said, shyly. It felt strange standing here in front of the man who was soon to become her husband, and yet, until this moment, they had never spoken a word to each other.

"We better get going if we are going to make good time today. I am hoping to travel at least twenty miles per day if weather permits."

"If you get that far, Mr. Bell, you *will* be making good time indeed," Mitchell chuckled.

"May I take your bag?" Jonah offered, holding out his hand to Savannah.

"Yes, thank you, sir." Savannah handed him her bag and reached to hug her mother for the last time. "I love you so," she whispered, and headed off the porch steps toward the wagon.

This was not the time to cry or look back at her mother, who she knew was crying as well. No longer was she a child, but a grown woman who was about to become a wife and instant mother to a newborn baby she'd yet to meet.

It was now time for her to put away her tears and allow God to carry her through the rest of her life.

*****

Savannah never once looked back as the wagon rounded the curve and headed west, a direction she'd not yet ventured. To look back, Savannah knew, would bring her a world of sadness, and she couldn't bear to see her mother on the porch watching her disappear.

Jonah helped her up on the wagon's seat beside him since the baby was sleeping, and now she sat quietly, with her hands folded on the long blue skirt her mother had made her yesterday, for her journey.

She only wished she was as good a seamstress as her mother and worried that Mr. Bell had no idea what he was getting himself into. Surely, he expected her to know everything there was to know about cooking, cleaning and raising children. But of course, she lacked greatly compared to what her mother knew.

And she was certain that Clara had known as much, also.

How would she ever compare?

*****

It seemed like eternity before daylight completely overtook the darkness, or maybe that was because Jonah didn't seem to know what to say, and Savannah wondered if he was perhaps waiting on her to speak first.

Never had she felt so awkward in all her life.

"What is your daughter's name, sir?" she asked, barely above a whisper.

"Rose. Her name is Rose." Jonah was glad Savannah had asked. For the life of him, he was struggling to find words to speak.

What he was doing was still a shock, even to him.

There was no turning back now, for everything was signed and what little belongings he was taking were packed.

"Rose is a beautiful name and my mother's favorite flower."

"It was Clara's favorite, too; that's why she named her Rose."

"I am truly sorry about your wife, Mr. Bell."

Jonah wondered if he should tell her that he wished not to speak of Clara. But then he *had* mentioned her first. And he certainly did not wish for his daughter to grow up and not know her real mother. How else would that happen if he never spoke of her?

Should he tell her not to ever expect to take Clara's place, and that the only reason he was marrying her was so that others wouldn't talk about her living so closely with him? That he could never love her.

Should he tell her that he never intended to touch her in an intimate way, because she could not possibly ever own his heart, for his heart was buried beside Clara on the land that now belonged to her father?

"It's going to be a good day for travel." Jonah knew best to change the subject. The last thing he wanted was to regret the move he was making to an unknown land with a total stranger and a baby he could hardly bear to touch.

"Yes sir, it shall be quite lovely, it seems."

Rose let out a loud cry, and Jonah pulled back on the reins. "Whoa!"

"I guess it's time for me to meet Rose," Savannah said, nervously.

"Yes, let me show you where things are." Jonah got down from the wagon and took Savannah's hand, helping her down also.

"It is easier to go in the wagon from the back than to crawl behind the seat with your long skirt."

Savannah followed Jonah to the back of the wagon. So far, he'd not looked once at her and she wondered why. Even on her parent's front porch, he had looked not at her face, but at her parents as they spoke.

Jonah reached in and took a stool out of the wagon and placed it on the ground below.

"Here, allow me." Jonah offered his hand to Savannah, helping her into the back of the covered wagon.

"I milked the goat this morning and strained the foam. The contents are in that jar, covered in cheesecloth to keep it cool.

There's a wooden spoon and cloth nappies, along with a few gowns that Clara made before......." His voice trailed off.

"Anyway, everything you need should be there. If you need me to stop for anything, let me know."

"Thank you, sir; we shall be fine."

Jonah set the stool back into the wagon and headed for the front. There were miles ahead, and it pained him to look at Savannah, and realize what he was about to do, to wed another woman when his heart belonged to Clara.

Savannah gently picked up the crying bundle, and removed the covers slowly to see Rose's face. "Shhh, sweet baby girl. I will feed you. Are you hungry?" Rose stopped crying the moment she was picked up.

Savannah placed the tiny infant in her lap and reached for the milk and wooden spoon. It wouldn't be easy spoon-feeding a baby who had been accustomed to nursing, but there was no other alternative.

She prayed last night the baby would be able to eat with no problem and get enough nourishment. After all, if something happened to Rose, where would that leave her? For Jonah's only interest in her at all was to be a caregiver for Rose.

"Come on, sweetheart; let's take a tiny sip of milk." Savannah gently tipped the spoon upwards and slowly let the goat's milk fall into Rose's mouth. Some of the milk seeped out the edge of her mouth, and Savannah caught it with the spoon and placed it back inside.

Over and over, Savannah let tiny bits of milk fall into Rose's mouth until Rose seemed to get the hang of it and would swallow the contents.

"That's wonderful, precious; you are getting the hang of it. You are just so tiny and adorable, little missy. That's the way, drink up, sweetie."

Jonah wiped at the tears in his eyes, hearing Savannah feed Rose. He was so afraid that Rose wouldn't take to the wooden spoon, and he might have to turn around and go back to Nelly, but from what he could hear coming from the back of the wagon, Savannah was feeding his tiny daughter with no trouble at all.

It wasn't easy hearing Savannah's sweet voice, knowing how much she sounded like his Clara. It should have been Clara's voice he was hearing. It should have been Clara in the back of their wagon holding Rose, the baby she was so thrilled to have when she found out she was carrying a child.

How could everything go so wrong?

Jonah almost decided to stay in Dahlonega after Clara passed, only because Rose needed milk that only Nelly could give her.

But the long nights were driving him mad, being there alone with only the sound of the wind outside to keep him company.

Rose was at the Bakers' house more and more, and even though Nelly offered for her to stay a few months until she could eat food, he knew that was something Clara would never have allowed.

He was handling Rose the best he could, but it pained him to hold her. Not that he blamed her entirely, but if she were not born, Clara would still be with him. It was something he knew he must work through.

One morning, two weeks after Clara passed, Jonah carefully placed a wooden cross he had carved on her grave.

How could he live in Dahlonega, Georgia when their plan was to travel west to the Arkansas Territory? They were so excited about moving there, staking their claim and raising more babies.

He remembered the last time he stood at her grave.

Oh, Clara, why did you leave me?

Jonah looked down at the dirt that was still fresh under his feet.

How could he stay, knowing her body lay here and not warm and alive and vibrant as she'd always been?

Jonah looked back at the small cabin they called their home. How could he continue to live there, knowing that is where she died, in the same place they'd made love so many times?

Jonah knew the pain would soon consume him, and the only thing left to do would be to fulfill their dream, if it was the last thing he ever did. All he needed was someone to take care of Rose while he was on the long journey there and afterwards. After all, he knew nothing about caring for something as tiny as his daughter; that was a mother's instinct, not a man's.

And yet now, after everything was set in place and his rough calloused hands held the reins tightly, he wondered if he was doing the right thing.

Was it right to have taken such a young girl so far away from the only family she ever knew, when he knew in his heart, he could never be a real husband to her?

Was it right to ruin what every young girl dreamt about; to have children of her own with a husband who loved her?

Jonah listened to Savannah's soothing voice as she sang to Rose and knew his daughter would grow up thinking of this young girl as her mother. She would never know the wonderful woman who gave birth to her, the woman who felt her kick and loved her with all her heart.

The pain Jonah felt was almost unbearable, and he wiped at another tear. The sweet song Savannah was singing was the same song he'd heard Clara singing to their baby while she was still in the womb.

Sometimes the memories were more than he could bear.

"Oh Jonah, come here quick and place your hand here," Clara said.

Jonah laughed and placed his hand on her round stomach. "Wow, he is a real strong little thing, isn't he?"

"Oh, Jonah, what if he is a she? Would you be terribly disappointed?"

Jonah kissed his beautiful wife on the lips and pulled her close. "As long as *she* is just like her mother, I think I can handle it."

Clara smiled. "Yes, as long as he or she is healthy, it doesn't matter what God blesses us with. I can't wait, Jonah, I am so excited to give birth to our baby and hold it in my arms."

"You are going to make a great mother, Clara."

"And you will make a great father. I can't wait to see our child following after you."

"Are you sure you want to leave Dahlonega?" Jonah asked again.

"Oh yes, we shall be able to leave right after the baby comes. I can nurse our child from anywhere. We need to leave so we can settle in before winter. Oh, Jonah, I can't wait to see the flat land and see the sun come over the horizon. I do love these mountains, but just think of the great farming land we shall have."

"It's a long journey, Clara. Are you sure you are up to it?"

Clara laughed. "I won't be this big and slow forever, Jonah, just wait. I shall be down to size again in no time."

"Mr. Bell, might I go relieve myself, please?" Savannah asked.

Jonah jumped as his thoughts came back to the moment. "Whoa," he said to the horses, pulling tight on the reins. "Yes, you may. I'm sorry; I should have stopped before now."

"That's okay, sir, it took me awhile to get Rose back to sleep, but she seems to be sleeping now."

Jonah jumped down and set the stool on the ground to help Savannah out of the wagon.

"Thank you for doing such a good job with Rose. I was afraid she wouldn't eat with a spoon."

"She is such a smart baby; she caught on quickly. I bet she will do everything early."

"Everything?" Jonah asked.

"Yes, like talk and walk. She is a smart one and catches on quickly to things."

"Oh, I see what you mean." Jonah looked around. "I think you might get some privacy over there," he pointed to a row of trees.

"Thank you, sir. I will return shortly."

"Take your time." Jonah watched Savannah walk toward the trees until she disappeared. It was the first time he'd *really* looked at her. She looked so much older than her age, almost twenty, in fact, and he wondered how close to seventeen she was. But then, what did it matter that she was beautiful? His heart could never belong to her. She was built so much like Clara that Jonah knew he must not look at her directly or the pain would be too much. And falling into temptation would be going against the vows he had made to the only woman he had ever loved.

"Thank you, sir," Savannah smiled, walking back to the wagon.

"As I said, I am sorry I haven't stopped before now. If you don't mind, I better do the same before we get started again. I'll be right back."

Savannah smiled and watched him go toward the trees. Never would she have thought that three days ago she would find herself here with the same man she had sneaked glances at, for so long, as she walked past to the mercantile while he was in the fields. So many times, she had felt guilty for thinking such thoughts about a married man.

Each night she had asked God to forgive her, and now God had placed her right into his hands. How strange that was. Maybe her mother was right; the Lord did work in mysterious ways.

24

CHAPTER 3

Jonah guided his horses toward the west, carrying everything he now owned. He hated leaving so many of the things he had obtained with Clara behind, like the large oak table he made her for Christmas. It had been her most prized possession.

He had also left behind their bed she loved, the bed she took her last breath in, the same bed Rose was conceived in. There were too many memories for him to drag it along, and not enough room.

It was time to have a fresh start in a new land. Jonah was strong and knew he could build a new cabin easily. It would be no problem to make a new table and chairs and two new beds, one for him and one for Savannah.

He brought along what there was room for, the things he couldn't bear to leave behind, like the quilts Clara had worked so hard on. He would never forget the long nights she would sit after dark by the lamplight and sew, thread by thread, until they were complete. "You do good work, Clara," Jonah said, pouring himself a cup of coffee. He loved watching his wife sew the quilt that would go on their bed.

Clara laughed. "You always tell me sweet things. Every girl knows how to sew; it's something we are taught at a young age."

"Well, you do it very well," he winked, leaning down to kiss her lips.

"How did I ever get so lucky to snag you for a husband?" she joked.

"It is I, the lucky one, and you know it."

"Is that right?"

Jonah sat down beside her at the table. "I wish I could give you more. You surely deserve much more."

"Jonah," Clara smiled the smile that made his heart melt. "You have given me much more than I ever hoped for. In fact, you have given me something that you don't even know about."

Jonah looked at his wife, puzzled. "And what is that, my beautiful wife?"

Clara smiled again. "Do you know how handsome you are in the lamplight?"

Jonah laughed. "Only the lamplight? What about the light of day?"

"In the light of day, my handsome husband, you are even more amazing."

Jonah chuckled. "You flatter me. So, tell me, what it is I am yet to know?"

Clara put down her sewing and stood. "Do I look like I've gained weight?"

Jonah looked at his slim wife and shook his head. "Not that I can see, why?"

"Because, if I have calculated right, I have been expecting your child for about three months now."

Jonah jumped to his feet, spilling his coffee. "You are going to have a baby!"

Clara laughed at his excitement. "I shall have your child early spring."

Jonah picked Clara up in his strong arms and spun her around. "Yippee! We are going to have a baby. Are you sure? Are you all right?"

"I am sure."

"We need to find a doctor to make sure everything is fine."

"Jonah, I don't need a doctor. I am only twenty-five and in perfect health. Nelly lives close enough that when the time comes, you can fetch her."

"But what if there are complications?"

Clara kissed Jonah tenderly. "Dear husband of mine, don't think negative. Nelly has had babies of her own and helped bring a few into this world. It will be a piece of cake."

Jonah shook his head trying to rid himself of the memories of that night. How could such a joyous thing turn so wrong?

How could he have known that in six short months his whole world would end? How could he have known he would never see Clara alive again, or never hold her in his arms?

*****

Jonah was proud of the distance they had traveled but felt sure the horses needed rest and water. The back of the wagon was quiet for some time, and he wondered what Savannah and Rose were up to.

Jonah stopped at a spot beside the river that looked ideal for camping and jumped off the wagon seat. The sun would be setting soon, and he dreaded what lay ahead, knowing he would have to make conversation with Savannah, feeling he would never be good company for anyone.

Jonah was never good at conversations with other women except Clara. It took him a while to get used to Nelly, but that was only because she was Clara's friend, and in and out all the time. How could he talk to such a young girl that he knew nothing about, knowing she would one day expect more from him than he could ever give?

Jonah pulled back the flap to the wagon to help Savannah out and froze. Savannah was lying on a bed of quilts sound asleep, with Rose cradled between her body and arm.

It was wrong to look upon another woman with lust in your heart. Isn't that what God's Word told us? Clara was not dead a month, and to think Savannah was beautiful disgusted him. After all, she was just a child. Just because she looked much older than her age did not make it so.

Unlike Clara with straight golden hair, Savannah's hair was dark and wavy, yet she was every bit as beautiful.

How he wished he could have chosen someone less beautiful, perhaps older than himself. That way he would never have to worry about the desires he felt sure would come as time went on, the curse of being a man.

Savannah opened her eyes and realized Jonah was standing at the opening of the wagon.

"Oh sir, I am so sorry I fell asleep. Please forgive me."

"Forgive you for falling asleep?"

Savannah sat up gently so as not to awaken Rose. "Yes sir, I am supposed to be tending your baby."

"Does that mean you shall never sleep again?" Jonah managed to smile.

Savannah chuckled, "I guess not. I didn't sleep very well last night, sir."

"Would it be all right if you call me Jonah?"

"Would that not be disrespectful, sir?"

"Why would calling me Jonah be disrespectful?"

"Because you are older than me, and my mother would be upset if I called an elder anything other than ma'am or sir."

Jonah shook his head and looked at her face for the first time as he spoke. He hadn't realized she would be so beautiful. "That may be true for just anyone, but surely not for someone that is going to be your husband. Is your father older than your mother?"

"Yes sir."

"And what does your mother call your father?"

"Mitchell. She calls him Mitchell."

Jonah shrugged. "Then I think she would be okay if you called me Jonah. Besides, it makes me feel old when you call me sir."

Savannah smiled, happy that Jonah was having a conversation with her. Still, it was hard to look him in the eyes. What if he figured out she'd had a crush on him since the first time she saw him plowing in the field, even before his wife died? He might think she was frivolous and not the marrying type.

"Yes sir, I mean Jonah. I shall try to remember to call you Jonah, please forgive me when I forget."

"You will get used to it in time. I think we shall camp here for the night. I am going to unhitch the horses and take them closer to the river to drink. After that I shall fetch some firewood and try to find some game, perhaps a rabbit or squirrel for dinner."

"What shall I do, sir?"

Jonah smiled at her and shook his head. "You forgot quickly."

"I'm so sorry, sir, oh, I mean Jonah." She turned a shade of red.

Jonah laughed. "Here, let me help you down so you can go relieve yourself. After that, you can get out the pans for cooking. Do you know how to cook?"

"Yes. I am not as good as Mother, but you will survive."

"Well, that is good to know. I guess I should have found all this out *before* I asked for your hand in marriage," he joked.

Savannah stepped out of the wagon, holding Jonah's calloused hand. "I see you have flour and meal, as well as eggs. I shall make you some fried bread."

"Sounds good. I shall bring meat as soon as I can. Will you be all right here? I won't go far."

"Yes, I shall be fine. I can unhitch the horses, if you like."

"You know how to do that?"

"Yes, my father taught me, since he didn't have a son. Now, with my brother being seven, I am sure he will teach him more than he ever taught me."

"Okay then, I will go fetch the game and wood."

"I can fetch the wood, too, Jonah. Rose should sleep a bit longer."

Jonah smiled. "I won't be long." He reached in the wagon to get his rifle, before heading toward the woods.

Jonah waited for a moment out of sight and watched her unhitch both horses and lead them to the edge of the river. She then came back for the small nanny goat and led her to the river also. It did not seem right, watching her do what he felt he should have done, but he wanted to show her that he trusted her to do as she said, to make her feel needed. The last thing he wanted to do was treat her as a child.

Perhaps she knew what she was doing, after all. Mitchell Bowen had taught his daughter well.

*****

Savannah gathered the last of the wood and placed it the way her father had always shown her before going after the iron skillet.

Rose was starting to whimper as Savannah climbed back into the wagon.

"Hi there, little one," Savannah said softly, picking her up and cradling her. "Are you hungry again?"

Rose was beautiful and reminded Savannah of a doll that her parents bought her for Christmas when she was just a small child. She treasured the porcelain-faced doll and left it back home for her sister, Mary, for when she was old enough to appreciate it.

"You must look just like your mother." Savannah took her tiny hand and rubbed it between her finger and thumb. "You are so beautiful and soft. I'm sorry you will have to settle for me, as

I am sure I won't even come close to the sort of mother your real mother would have been, but I promise to do my very best."

Savannah placed a spoonful of goat's milk into Rose's eager mouth. "You are such a smart girl and so precious."

"You are good with her," Jonah said, looking in the wagon.

"Oh, you startled me," Savannah laughed.

"I'm sorry; you were talking and didn't hear me come up. Would this be all right for dinner?" Jonah held up two rabbits.

"You are a good hunter; that didn't take long at all."

"I got lucky. I will clean them down by the river and we shall save the fur to dry. It makes good trading, for corn meal and flour."

"Yes, my father trades skins all the time. I will start the bread as soon as she is settled. She must eat more often since she isn't nursing."

"Do you think she will make it?" Jonah worried that his tiny daughter wouldn't get the nourishment she needed to survive.

"Of course, she will; she seems strong enough, and she's eating well."

"That's good. I worry about her."

"You have a very beautiful little girl who seems to be healthy."

Jonah smiled at her. Maybe he *had* made the right decision. "Thank you. I shall go and skin our dinner."

*****

Dark was fast approaching as Savannah washed the iron skillet at the edge of the river. The fried bread and potatoes turned out well with the rabbit, but she wondered if Jonah already regretted taking her to wed. Surely her cooking didn't compare to Clara's. She looked back toward the wagon and watched Jonah pour himself a cup of coffee and sit down on the ground to lean against the wagon's wheel.

How handsome he was, so deep in thought, and Savannah wondered what was on his mind.

He hardly said two words during dinner and she guessed he was still grieving the loss of his beloved wife. But why wouldn't he be? It was not even a month yet.

Savannah saw Jonah look her way and nod.

He was polite enough, and Savannah appreciated him trying hard to make her feel included.

"Thank you for dinner; it was tasty," Jonah complimented, as Savannah came close enough to hear.

"Thank you. I will get better as time goes on."

"Nothing wrong with it now. We shall reach the church tomorrow afternoon and have the parson marry us."

Savannah nodded her approval.

"I'm sorry that you didn't have a choice in this."

"My father liked you."

Jonah took a sip of coffee and looked at her in thought. He wondered how she felt about being traded for land. "Did he?"

"Yes, he said you were a good man."

Jonah nodded. "Still, you had no choice in the matter. Can I ask you something?"

"Yes."

"Do you even *want* to marry me?"

Savannah stood, speechless. How could she tell him he was the only man she would have ever wished to marry?

"I guess that answers my question," he chuckled, after a few moments of silence.

"Jonah, I know you still love Clara, and I understand why you are marrying me."

"Do you?"

"Yes, you are marrying me out of honor because you need someone to take care of Rose. If you don't wish to marry me, we don't have to tell anyone we are not married. No one will ever know."

"And yet that would be a lie. Savannah, I feel that it's best to tell you now, that I *do* still love Clara. I am not sure I will make a very good husband, as husbands go, when my heart will belong to her, and only her. I feel I have done you an injustice by dragging you along. The only one of us that will benefit is me, for I shall have someone to tend Rose, but where does that leave you?"

"I am not sure what to say," she shrugged. "I don't mind taking care of that precious child, she is beautiful, and I don't mind becoming your wife, if that is what you desire. I am soon to be seventeen and way above the marrying age. If anything, we shall become great friends."

Jonah smiled. Just as he thought, she not only looked older than her age, but she was wise beyond her years, as well.

"Then we shall wed tomorrow. Don't worry, though; I don't plan to consummate this marriage, at least as long as Clara still owns so much of my heart. I hope you will understand."

"I understand. Besides, I have never known a man in that way and am in no hurry to rush things. But should the time ever come that you desire me in that way, I shall be your wife and it will be my duty to fulfill your desire." Savannah didn't stay to hear his response; instead, she headed for the back of the wagon to check on Rose and place the pan away.

Jonah liked her spunk and knew she could be someone he could easily have fallen for if not for the circumstances. As far as the way he felt at the moment, the last thing he desired was a new love.

Setting down his tin cup, he rose to light the lanterns. It would be completely dark soon, and they would need light.

Savannah was feeding Rose when he climbed into the wagon. "Let me light the lantern; you will need it soon."

"Thank you. Do you plan to leave again before daybreak?"

"We would make better time that way. Since you made extra bread, we won't have to wait to eat breakfast."

"When we camp tomorrow, I will need to wash Rose's nappies. I'm sorry I didn't think about that this evening."

"Will she have enough to do her until then?"

"Yes, she should have plenty. Would you like to hold her a bit?"

Jonah pulled back. "Not while she is eating."

"It's fine. I will show you how to feed her."

"No. I'm going to get my bed roll and get ready for bed." Jonah picked up one of the lanterns and a bed roll and headed out of the wagon.

Savannah was confused. She'd been with him since before daybreak, and not once had she seen him hold his daughter. How could they form a bond if he never held her? Jonah had issues that went way beyond missing his wife.

As tired as she was from not sleeping the night before, Savannah lay awake for the longest thinking about the journey ahead and what was in store for her.

This was her last night as a Bowen. Come tomorrow, she would be a mother to the most precious daughter, and a wife to a man who would always be in love with a memory.

Perhaps she could write a bit in her journal before closing her eyes.

Who would have ever guessed I would be asked by Jonah Bell to become his wife? My heart aches for him because I can see the pain he is still bearing for Clara.

How shall I ever be able to fill her shoes?

It has been a very long and tiring day and as I write this by the light of Jonah's lantern, I must wonder what Mother is doing now. Usually she would be reading us passages from her Bible, but she gave it to me. Whatever shall she read now?

I have so many emotions surging inside of me, so many things I have yet to imagine.

What shall it be like to be Jonah's wife and Rose's mother? What does the land look like in Arkansas?

Shall I be able to make our cabin a home the way Mother made ours?

Tomorrow my last name will change to Bell, and even though there is a part of me that is so afraid for this new adventure, the other part of me feels giddy.

Why do I feel ashamed for writing this, my feelings, and know that if it wasn't for Clara's death, this would never have happened to me at all?

Oh, tell me how shall I compete with a ghost?

Savannah lay down her journal and looked at Rose, who slept peacefully. She snuggled down under the beautiful quilt Clara had made and wondered if Jonah slept as peacefully outside the wagon.

*****

Jonah lay awake and counted the stars. The light inside the wagon had gone out an hour before, and he knew Savannah and Rose were now sleeping.

What was he thinking to bring them both out west to chase after a dream?

Was this what he *really* wanted, or was he trying to keep Clara alive by fulfilling her dream?

Savannah was so accommodating and helpful; the last thing he wanted to do was hurt her, yet he knew in his heart he was bound to do just that.

How could he tell her that he couldn't bear to hold his own daughter, or ever hold her as a man should hold his wife?

How could he rid himself of the feelings he felt deep inside his soul, that Rose played a part in Clara's death, and even though he knew it wasn't her fault, these feelings wouldn't allow him to bond, as a father should.

Besides, Rose was the spitting image of her mother, and to look at her was much too painful.

"I miss you, Clara," Jonah whispered. "Are you up there looking down?"

Jonah pulled the quilt close to rid the chill, wondering what Clara would think of another woman sleeping in their wagon.

The night grew cold with the wind, but it wouldn't be proper for him to sleep in the wagon. It would be time to leave, soon enough.

Tomorrow, he would no longer be Clara's husband. Savannah would take his last name. Yet still, he knew he would continue sleeping on the ground outside the wagon during their journey. How could he ever lay down with a woman who wasn't Clara?

Jonah closed his eyes, willing morning to arrive faster.

Ever since Clara's death there was nothing he hated more than the dark.

CHAPTER 4

The movement of the wagon jolted Savannah awake. It was still dark, and Jonah was already heading west.

With each passing mile, her home and family were getting farther away, but then Jonah and Rose were her family now; oh, how very strange that felt.

It felt strange holding Rose and kissing her tiny hands, knowing that she would grow up thinking of her as a mother, and she hoped she would be as good a mother as her own, instilling in her values and teaching her about God.

Savannah had grown up listening to her mother tell her Bible stories and read verses from her Bible, the same Bible she would read to Rose.

Rose whimpered, and Savannah sat up and reached for the milk. It was warm. Jonah must have already milked the goat and strained it. How could he have finished so much right under her nose, as she slept?

"Jonah," Savannah said, loud enough for him to hear.

"Yes?"

"You should have awakened me, so I could have helped you. I am capable of milking."

"It's all right, we have a long journey ahead of us, and there will be plenty of time for you to help. Besides, I couldn't sleep."

"I didn't sleep well, either."

"Were you warm enough?"

"Yes, thank you. Just nervous, I guess."

"Why are you nervous?" Jonah asked, already knowing the answer, for he was feeling the same jitters in the pit of his stomach.

"I've never been married before, Jonah." There, she said it. It was easier to talk to him when she didn't have to look into his face and speak. Here inside the wagon with him just a few feet from her, she knew he could hear her well.

"Are you sure you want to marry me?" Jonah wasn't so sure himself.

"Yes."

"I'm sorry your parents won't be there. I guess I left in such a hurry I didn't plan this well."

"It's all right. I might have been more nervous had they been there."

Jonah didn't answer. His mind wandered to the day he had wed Clara.

It was a hot summer day. Clara was beautiful in her white dress she'd made herself. Her blonde hair was pinned on top of her head. Her eyes were like crystal, and Jonah lost himself each time he looked into the depths of them.

"Are you two kids sure you are ready to tie the knot?" Bert Walton laughed. He'd been the parson in their small town for a number of years.

"We are hardly kids," Jonah teased back. "It just took me a while to convince her that she couldn't live without me."

"Oh, Jonah," Clara laughed. "It was the other way around, Mr. Walton, and he knows it."

"Well, let's get this thing over with then," Bert winked. "Are you planning on staying here in Savannah close to the coast?"

"No sir," Jonah said, proudly. "I'm taking this pretty thing to Dahlonega. I hear it's beautiful there in the northeast Georgia mountains."

"Never been that far north. Could take you a week of traveling."

"That's what we guess. We can have a honeymoon on the way," Jonah winked at Clara and made her blush.

Clara slapped at Jonah's arm. "Jonah, this is a parson you are talking to."

Marrying Clara was the best decision he ever made. Why did God take her away so soon? Until the night she died, he believed in a mighty God, and now trying to think about a loving God only angered him. It was all a lie, a lie he believed for much too long.

Jonah knew that within three hours, they would reach the church where he would meet a new parson and marry Savannah. Today was not the time to be thinking of Clara, or he would never be able to go through with it.

*****

"The parson is waiting on us," Jonah said, holding his hand out to help Savannah from the wagon. "There is still time if you'd rather not do this. I wouldn't want to force you to do anything you are not comfortable with."

Savannah took his hand and stepped from the wagon, holding onto Rose with the other arm. "The question is, are *you* ready?" she whispered, looking into his eyes, knowing he'd rather be anywhere than here.

"It's the right thing to do," he nodded. "Are you going to take Rose?"

"She is awake, and we can't leave her alone in the wagon."

"Yes, I guess not. I was not thinking."

Savannah had never wanted her mother as bad as she did at this moment.

She followed along behind Jonah to the small church, carrying Rose, wondering if her blue skirt was all right for getting married in. It was the best she had.

Was this the plan God had for her? Was it His will that she marry Jonah Bell and be a mother to Rose and wife to him?

Did God *really* want her to marry a man who would *never* love her?

Oh Mother, how I wish you were here today. How I wish you could give me advice as you always have. As bad as I have wanted to grow up and be a woman, I am not sure that I am ready at all.

"Isn't that a sweet thing?" an older woman said, as they entered the church. "I'm Sara Howington, David's wife. Please allow me to hold ye little one while ye two joins together as husband and wife. Looks like ye should have done that first," she laughed.

"Rose is not my daughter, ma'am." Savannah felt silly trying to explain herself, but it wasn't proper to have a child before wedlock.

"My wife passed a month ago, and Savannah has agreed to marry me and take care of my daughter."

Sara took Rose out of Savannah's arms. "None of my business one way or the other. David!" Sara called out.

A tall slender man walked out from the back room of the church. "Yes, Sara?"

"They are ready."

"That's wonderful, come, come," he motioned.

Jonah looked at Savannah and nodded before taking her hand and walking to the front of the church.

"Well, well, you two do make a fine-looking couple. Marriage is not to be taken lightly. It is the joining of one man and one woman in Holy wedlock. Please state your full name for me, sir."

"Jonah Andrew Bell."

"Jonah, do you take this woman to be your lawfully wedded wife, to have and to hold, from this day forward, forsaking all others; in sickness and in health, for better or worse, richer or poorer, till death do you part?"

Jonah looked at the dark-haired young girl before him. She was indeed beautiful, but how did he get here? Was it not so long ago he stood before another altar with the love of his life, his golden-haired Clara?

David cleared his throat and brought Jonah back to the present.

"Yes, yes I do."

"Please state your full name, ma'am."

"Savannah Elizabeth Bowen."

"Do you, Savannah, take this man to be your lawfully wedded husband, to have, to hold, and to obey, from this day forward, forsaking all others, in sickness and in health, for better or worse, richer or poorer, as long as you both shall live?"

"I do," she whispered.

"Speak louder, dear," David asked.

"I do," she said, louder, staring Jonah in the face, certain he could see her trembling. "Well, then, by the power vested in me, in the state of Georgia, I now pronounce you husband and wife. Jonah, you may kiss your bride."

Jonah breathed in deeply. He'd never kissed anyone but his beloved Clara, and yet here he stood in front of two witnesses, with nothing left to do.

Lightly he pressed his lips to Savannah's just as Rose let out an earsplitting scream.

Sara laughed. "I guess she's had enough of this."

Savannah hurried toward Sara, and took Rose gently from her hand. "Thank you for holding her."

"You are welcome. Congratulations, you two."

"Thank you," Jonah willed himself to smile. "Are you ready to go?"

"Yes," Savannah nodded. She felt as if she were suffocating and needed the fresh air.

"Hold on," David yelled out, holding a piece of paper. "Don't forget your marriage license." He handed Jonah the paper and clucked his tongue. "Never seen anyone in such a hurry before," he joked.

"Thanks again." Jonah shook his hand and placed the license in his pocket.

As the wagon pulled away from the small white church and Savannah watched it disappear, she breathed a sigh of relief, glad that it was over.

For as long as she would live, she would keep the picture of it in her mind. A place she married the man she once thought she would never have. For now, she knew it would only be his heart she could never own.

Somehow, she had pictured her wedding day totally different. All her life she had dreamed of her wedding being a fairy-tale kind of day, with flowers, and standing by a man who loved her with all his heart. Her father would walk her down the aisle and give her away. But then, in a strange sort of way, her father *had* given her away. He had traded her for one hundred acres.

*****

"May I come sit with you a spell, so I can see the land?" Savannah asked, crawling over the seat of the wagon.

"I could have stopped," Jonah answered. "It's not proper for a lady to crawl over a wagon seat in a skirt."

Savannah laughed. "Don't tell that to my father—not sure he ever heard that. Besides, it isn't hard to crawl over."

Savannah loved being able to see the beautiful mountains they were leaving behind. She was tired of riding in the back of the covered wagon, when there was so much to see in front of them.

"Is Rose sleeping?"

"Yes, her belly is full, and she's fast asleep."

"I can't believe she is eating so well." That was such great news to Jonah.

"Yes, it's a process with a spoon, but I guess God is teaching me patience."

"You are a great mother. I'm only sorry that you were forced into this, especially since you are such a young age."

"Almost seventeen is not *that* young."

"This is true. Yet still, you've become an instant mother overnight."

"I've dreamed of becoming a mother, since I can remember."

Jonah looked her way for a brief second and said nothing to the comment. He wondered how she would feel knowing she would never be able to have babies of her own.

"Do you really think Rose is going to make it? Does she seem strong enough to you?"

"She seems very healthy and has a huge appetite."

"And that is good, I guess?"

"It is great. But I must wash her nappies at the next river we come to."

"I remember when Clara made all her nappies. I traded rabbit fur for the material. She made Rose's gowns from flour sacks."

"She did beautiful work." Savannah wasn't sure what to say when speaking of Clara.

She wasn't sure how much he wished to talk about her, but oh, how she so wanted to ask him so many questions about his late wife and about their life together, knowing it would help her understand him better.

"She did. Do you sew, Savannah?"

"I've been sewing since I was a small child. My mother told me that every woman must learn to sew."

"That's good," he chuckled. "I always get holes in my socks."

Savannah shook her head and smiled. "My father always did, too. Socks are easy. I shall mend them for you."

"It won't be long, and we will be approaching a place where we can stop and get a few supplies. I have several skins that I can trade. Is there anything you would like to have?"

"If it shan't be too much trouble, I would like a bit of paper."

"Paper?" Jonah asked.

"Yes, I'm keeping a journal along the journey, so I shall never forget it in years to come."

"So, you read and write well, then?"

"Yes, my mother taught me to read and write also."

"Guess mine were too busy farming to care if I learned to read or write."

"I could teach you, if you like." Savannah couldn't imagine the torment of not being able to read or write.

"I haven't found that I need it very much. If I can hook up a plow and plant a field, hunt and fish and build a cabin, I will be fine. Signing my name is about the limit to my writing abilities."

"Would you like me to read to you? I cannot imagine not being able to read God's Word."

"Clara used to read it to me each night. I have heard God's Word but now realize it was lies, a book of fantasy."

"Lies?" Savannah was startled by his comment.

"Yes, lies. How can God be a God of love and take a life as young as Clara's right after she gave birth to our daughter? Why would he take Rose's mother away from her?"

Savannah looked up at the blue sky above and silently prayed that God would give her the words to speak to this man who was so bitter and still so in love with his late wife.

"I have never lost someone I loved, Jonah, and I couldn't imagine the pain you must have felt, and still feel. But when I view death, I like to think about it as God's way of rewarding us to come back to Him. I think for the person that passes it will be joyous and something that our natural bodies can't sustain. It only hurts the person that is left behind."

"Yes, it hurts very badly. But I'm sure if Clara had been given the chance to make her own decision, she would have wanted to stay and raise our daughter."

"I'm sorry, Jonah. I wish it was Clara that was sitting with you now and traveling west with you and Rose to live out your dream. I am sorry that it is I, and not the woman you love."

"We don't always get what we want."

"No, we don't. I will never understand the ways of God."

"I don't believe in God any longer, Savannah."

"It's okay, Jonah."

Jonah couldn't believe she would give up so easily. It wasn't like a woman to give up on something she believed in. "So, it doesn't matter that I no longer believe in God?"

"No," she smiled, "because He still believes in you."

*****

Savannah burped Rose and wrapped her tightly in the blanket Clara had crocheted from the softest yarn.

Jonah pulled into town and tied the horses. "I'll be back as soon as I can to fetch you."

Savannah nodded, knowing if he was like her father he had gone into the saloon for a drink. Of course, so far, he was nothing like her father. But where else could he have gone?

It pained Savannah at times when she thought of her earthly father. Mitchell Bowen was not a man she would ever wish her husband to be like. Even though he was the man God had sent to raise her, there were times she felt sorry for her mother because of the way he always spoke to her and ordered her around as if she were his slave.

It was true the man was to be the head of the household by God's law, yet still, Savannah grew up dreaming that she would fall in love with a man who was much kinder and gentler than her father had been to her mother.

Alice Bowen, on the other hand, was the best mother any girl could have asked for, and she had grown up thanking God for her daily. Oh, how hard it would be for her mother now with two small children and her not there to help. How would she ever get the loneliness of missing her mother out of her heart?

Perhaps there was time after she fed Rose for her to write a short poem to describe how she was feeling before Jonah came back.

*****

A dream so big, will I ever fit in
To raise a girl with a great big grin.
I had to marry because it wouldn't be right
If I should be seen with a man in God's sight.
Sunrises come, sunrises go,
But this was the last my mother would show.
A kind face and strong hands,
Traded for one hundred acres was the plan.
Roses are red, the sky is blue,
Mother's favorite flower is about to bloom.
We were married 1,2,3......
It wasn't so long ago, I hid behind that tree.

The guilt I feel for liking a married man,
Now he takes my married hand.
A friend I will be, for that is my lot,
Maybe never to taste the marriage cot.
A handsome man he is to me,
Full of pain for missing his wife,
What is God's plan in this adventure called life?

****

"Are you ladies ready?" Jonah smiled, looking into the wagon.

"Yes," Savannah nodded, realizing he'd gone to the barber for a haircut and shave.

"Sorry I was gone so long, but I knew it would take you a while to feed Rose."

"That's okay, it does take a while. You are just in time."

Jonah extended his hand and helped her from the wagon. "After we are finished here, we will find somewhere to camp tonight close to the river, so we can wash our clothes and take a bath. Have you ever bathed in the river before?"

"I have." Savannah pulled Rose close and followed Jonah toward the mercantile.

"I will buy some lye soap and get your paper and more flour and meal and sugar."

The mercantile was crowded with people. Savannah held her head high, knowing that everyone thought she was Jonah's wife and Rose's mother. How long would it take to get used to that?

How strange, it was just a week ago she was hiding behind a huge oak spying on him as he came by, and now, here she was, standing in a mercantile with him as his wife.

"Is there something I can help you with?" the proprietor asked, from behind the counter.

"Yes, I would like to do some trading, if I might," Jonah handed him the rabbit furs.

"Nice, I think we can do business. What is it you need?"

"We need one bar of lye soap, a sack of flour, meal and sugar and paper. Also, a couple dozen eggs and dried beans."

"Okay, give me just a moment and let me gather your things."

Jonah looked back at Savannah and saw her looking at a bolt of cloth with yellow flowers. "How many yards do you need?"

"It would make a cute dress for Rose."

"And what about you?"

"Oh, I don't need such luxuries; I have enough clothes to do me a while. But Rose could use a few more things. A couple of yards should do it."

Jonah was a kind man, and Savannah knew he would make any woman a wonderful husband but had no idea what was required of her to make him fall in love.

Perhaps there was no formula for love; it was just something that happened between two people when the time was right, and unfortunately, there were times that it was never right.

Not everyone was meant to be together. Not everyone was meant to fall in love.

Savannah walked across the planks of the wooden floor. She'd never seen a floor that shone as this one did.

There were so many pretty things to look at. The mercantile in Dahlonega didn't have as many things to choose from. Her eyes caught sight of a globe made of glass. She picked it up carefully and inspected it.

"Do you want it?" Jonah asked.

Savannah jumped and put the globe down. "Oh no, as I said, I don't need luxuries, but thank you."

"It's called a snow dome. I bought Clara one last Christmas, but unfortunately, I left it behind. I guess your father will find it and perhaps give it to your mother."

"She has never had such luxuries, either, so I am sure she will like it, if that be the case."

Jonah nodded sadly and walked back toward the counter.

"You have a beautiful baby," an attractive woman said, behind her. She was dressed in a dress that fit her so snugly it left nothing to the imagination.

"Thank you." There was no use trying to explain to everyone that Rose wasn't hers. She was now her stepmother, and she was certainly old enough to have given birth to her.

"Are you from around here? I don't remember seeing you before." She fanned herself with the decorative fan she held.

"No ma'am, we are just passing through, on our way to the Arkansas Territory."

"Why would you want to go so far away?"

"Jonah wants to build a cabin and settle down there; it's good land for farming."

The woman laughed and looked toward Jonah. "If you like that sort of thing, I guess. Wherever did you find him?"

"Excuse me?" Savannah wasn't sure what she meant, but from her tone knew it to be a snide remark, as if she wasn't good enough for Jonah.

"That fine-looking man. He *is* your husband, right?"

"Yes, he is." Savannah looked toward Jonah and saw him talking to the proprietor. She knew he was a handsome man but didn't like other women looking at him the way this woman did.

"Forgive me, but how old are you?" she looked back at Savannah from head to toe as if sizing her up.

49

"Twenty-two," Savannah lied, praying the Lord would forgive her. Why did she feel it necessary to defend herself? After all, Jonah *did* ask her to be his wife.

She laughed. "If you are twenty-two, then I am forty. No, I'd say you might be eighteen, but I highly doubt it."

"I guess it doesn't really matter, does it? That fine man is *my* husband," Savannah scoffed and walked away from her. Never had she been rude to anyone before now, but it angered her the way this woman made her feel.

"They will load our things in the wagon. Are you ready to go, or would you like to look more?" Jonah asked.

"I am ready," she nodded, and followed Jonah out of the mercantile, taking one last smug look at the woman, who was watching them leave.

Savannah wondered if Jonah would have ever been interested in a woman such as that. Maybe someday, when he realized she could never capture his heart, he would go looking elsewhere, but why was she thinking such thoughts? Her mother had taught her to be positive, and thinking such depressing thoughts was not good for her at all.

"We are what we say we are," her mother said time and time again. Or *"Don't speak it into existence."* She would never forget those words as long as she still had breath to breathe.

CHAPTER 5

Savannah stirred up the corn meal and goat's milk to fry. They would be good with the dried beans Jonah had purchased. She was glad her mother had taught her how to cook. Hopefully, after they were settled in their new cabin, she would be able to try different recipes; as for now, she was limited to what she could do with minimal supplies and a camp fire.

Jonah found a beautiful place to camp by the river, early enough for the beans to cook and both to get baths and wash the nappies.

Savannah had placed the beans in the pot to cook before she took her bath, and now, as she fried the bread, Jonah had gone to do the same.

It was a beautiful day to be married, a day Savannah knew she would never forget as long as she lived. Even if she was married to a man she knew may never love her. For her, he would be a man she could easily love. And if one of them loved the other, then perhaps that is all one needed.

The goat, which she'd named Betsy, let out a loud, Baaaa, and Savannah jumped. A rattlesnake crawled between her and the small goat and coiled around ready to strike. Savannah screamed, having no time to move, just as the gunshot went off, sending the snake flying backwards under the wagon.

"Are you okay?" Jonah asked, running towards her.

Savannah placed her hand over her heart and breathed in heavy. "Oh, my goodness, I have never been so scared. Did you kill it?"

"Looks that way. Have you ever eaten rattlesnake?" he grinned.

"No, I haven't, have you?"

"I have. It's quite good, actually, and the skin will be great for trading."

"You are a very good shot. Where did you learn to do that?"

"Been practicing since I was a small boy. Not much good for anything else but farming and shooting. Got me a new Harper's Ferry Conversion Percussion Rifle, so I am good to go," he winked.

"If you hadn't seen it, it would have bitten me. I hate snakes!"

"Most are harmless. That one, however, is not. I'm glad I was watching you fry the bread."

"Yes, I am glad you were, and thank you so much." She wondered why he would be watching her fry bread but thankful he was.

"You are welcome. It smells good; I am sure it will be tasty."

"I do hope you're right. I am frying some extra bread for breakfast; I know you like to start early."

"Good idea. We have a long way to go, and I want to have a small cabin built before winter sets in."

"I understand. I am anxious to see somewhere other than Georgia. I've never been more than three miles from Dahlonega."

"Really?" That amazed him, knowing how much he'd traveled.

"Yes, it was my father that always went farther than town. He said we were too much trouble to drag along."

"I used to live in Savannah, by the ocean."

Savannah smiled. "There's a town with *my* name?"

"There is. It's very beautiful there, with all the weeping willows that stand so tall, their branches dragging right to the ground."

"Why did you come to Dahlonega?"

"After Clara and I were married, we moved with a dream of finding gold."

"And did you?"

Jonah chuckled, "As I said, all I am really good at is farming and shooting. After a year, we decided when Rose was born, we would go to Arkansas to the flatter land to farm. She was as excited about the move as I was."

"I'm sorry, Jonah. I'm sorry your plans didn't work out."

Jonah picked up the rattlesnake and started for the river. "They did work out, just not the way I thought they would."

Savannah watched him go, carrying the snake. It was easy to see Jonah was so filled with pain, pain that she feared he may never be able to quench. So much so, that he had stopped believing in God.

Was this the reason, perhaps, that God placed her with him? Surely, in the years to come, she could convince him otherwise.

But how, dear Lord, how can that be? Please show me.

*****

Thunder rolled in the distance as the sky blackened.

For the past hour, Jonah could see the storm fast approaching from the east, so he tied the livestock to a sturdy oak nearby.

"Look at the sky," Savannah said, coming out of the wagon, holding her bonnet down to keep the wind from blowing it off.

"Going to be a powerful storm; I think I have everything secure enough."

"Do you think we are safe here? My Pa always took us to the storm shelter in weather such as this."

"Don't see as we have much of a choice."

Savannah looked up once again at the sky and shuddered. The thought of being caught in a tornado frightened her. "How long do you think the storm will last?"

"Can't rightly say—hopefully not long. Would it offend you if I slept in the wagon tonight if I promise to keep my distance?"

"You can't stay out in this weather, Jonah; besides, I am your wife now."

"Only on paper," he commented, placing the pots and pans back inside the wagon as quickly as possible.

Savannah kept quiet. Why had those words stung so badly? Would she have to go through every day of the rest of her life with him reminding her that their marriage would never mean anything?

Thunder rolled, and a crack of lightning close to the wagon caused Savannah to scream and jump.

"Better get in the wagon," Jonah motioned her forward, taking her hand to help her inside.

"Thank you, it's getting close. I hope we are safe."

Jonah felt her hand tremble from fright. Hopefully, it would be over soon; he didn't like being so close to her, especially with her being afraid. "We are safe enough, don't worry."

"Do you think I should hold Rose?"

"She's sleeping well; let's let her be for now." Jonah lit the oil lamp and closed the flap to the wagon entrance. "Gonna be monstrous, I'm afraid."

The pounding rain began to fall by the buckets, and another crack of thunder boomed above them, causing Savannah to jump again.

She could feel her heart racing. If she were home, she would be going with her parents and siblings to the storm shelter. Surely this wagon couldn't be safe.

"Are you sure we are safe?" she asked again.

"I'm hoping so. As of now, we don't have a choice on moving."

"Would you mind if I pray?"

Jonah said nothing for a moment. How many nights had Clara taken his hand and prayed out loud? Not a day went by that he had not heard his beautiful wife pray for their needs and thank God for their bountiful blessings.

Jonah nodded for her to proceed. Anything to make her feel less afraid. If praying to a God that did not exist made her less afraid, then so be it.

Savannah smiled faintly, and with all her courage, reached over and took his hands in hers before closing her eyes.

"Dear Father, thank You for bringing us thus far, safely. Thank you for Rose's healthy appetite. We trust she will continue to thrive and grow into the woman You wish for her to be. Lord, we ask now that You send Your angels to guard us and protect us from this storm and keep us safe in Your loving care. In Jesus' name, we pray, Amen."

Jonah looked at her, feeling tears pooling in his eyes. Her hands were small, just as Clara's had been.

"Thank you; that was beautiful."

"Even though you no longer believe in God?"

Jonah wiped at his eyes and avoided the question. "You are so much like Clara."

"I'm like Clara?" Savannah knew they looked nothing alike.

"The relationship you have with God. The way you pray. Clara prayed about everything."

"Are you a Christian, Jonah? Were you a Christian before you stopped believing in God?"

"I was."

She smiled. "God's Word tells us that He shall never leave us nor forsake us, which means He is still in there."

Jonah turned loose of her hands and pulled away from her. "I do not wish to talk about God."

The wagon rocked hard from the wind as the rain poured. The wind beat against the wagon's material and made a popping noise.

"This doesn't seem like a good time to not believe in God, but I will honor your wishes. So, what would you like to talk about?" she smiled. "Maybe that would keep our mind off the storm."

Jonah looked deeply into her eyes in wonder. Didn't anything upset her? Shouldn't she be furious that her father traded her for land, or that he never intended to be anything other than a friend?

He lay back against the flap of the wagon, trying to get as far away as possible. "I'm afraid I've never been much for talking."

"I'm sorry," Savannah said, biting her lip.

"For what?"

"My father used to call me a rattle box. He said I never know when to stop."

Jonah chuckled. "Clara was a rattle box, too. I guess that's all a part of being a woman."

Savannah nodded, after thinking it over. "My father wasn't much of a talker, either. Maybe you are right."

Jonah studied her for a moment in the lamplight, so beautiful. Perhaps she was every bit as beautiful as Clara was.

"Are you sure you won't resent me for taking you away from your family? Your mother looked powerful sad."

"I shall miss her greatly, as well as my brother and sister. But, as a woman, I knew the time would come I would have a family of my own."

Had he not made it clear to her that there would not be any more children, he thought.

"Do you think Rose shall think of me as her mother?" Savannah asked.

Jonah looked heartbroken. "I am sure; you will be the only woman she ever knows. I do want to tell her about her real mother, though. I think I owe that to Clara."

"Of course, you should." Savannah looked toward the sleeping bundle and wondered how she could sleep with such racket going on outside.

"If I had not asked for your hand in marriage, Savannah, who do you think you would have married? Did you have your eye on anyone particular?"

She wondered where that came from. How could she tell him that he was the only one she *ever* had her eye on, without him thinking badly of her, since he had been a married man at the time. "I suppose I might not have ever gotten married, there were so few men in the area that wasn't already."

"So, you didn't think anyone at your school was special?"

Savannah giggled. "They were all so childish; I could not imagine ever being married to any of them."

"So, then I saved you?" he joked, trying to get her mind off the storm and make light of their situation.

She smiled. "I guess you did."

The darkness closed in around them as the storm raged and the wagon shook. Rose stretched and yawned but never woke up.

"Looks like she can sleep through anything, just like her mother."

"It's better that she does; the storm is so scary."

"Guess we better get some shut-eye; morning comes early. Are you sure you don't mind me sleeping in the wagon tonight?"

"Jonah, you have no other choice; you would drown out there."

He nodded in agreement. "True, but there's not much room in here. I can sleep sitting up like this."

"Don't be silly; you need your rest. There is plenty of room for us side by side here in the middle of the wagon. I promise, I will not bite you." Savannah lay down and scooted over as much as possible.

Jonah crawled to the other side and lay down beside her. He never intended to have to sleep next to her, but the storm left him no other option. "And I promise not to bite you." He reached over and turned down the wick of the oil lamp, causing the wagon to grow completely dark.

"Could I ask a favor?" Savannah said, faintly. "When I was little, and the storms were so bad outside, my mother used to crawl in bed behind me and place her arm around me. Do you think it would be okay if you put just one arm over me?"

Jonah froze. What was she asking? Did she not realize the effect she had on him with her beauty? Was she so innocent that she had no idea what that would do to a man? How would Clara feel if she knew another woman could have such an effect on him in such a short amount of time?

Savannah heard his breathing change. Had she insulted him by asking too much? "I'm sorry, Jonah, I should not have asked. Please forgive me."

"It's okay; I don't see any harm in that." Jonah slid closer to her and put his arm around her. He could literally feel his heart pounding in his chest. She felt so warm and small in his arms, just as Clara had.

"Thank you, Jonah. It always comforts me."

Jonah could feel the sweat bead up on his forehead. Surely, she could feel his heart pounding against her back. "How long do you think Rose will sleep?" he asked, trying to talk about anything but the obvious.

"She should sleep another couple of hours. I will try not to wake you when I feed her, but I will have to turn the lamp back on."

"That's okay, I will get up with you for a while; we can always go back to sleep when she does. You have done a fine job with her, Savannah, and I thank you."

She smiled in the darkness and pressed even closer to him. It felt so wonderful to be held by him. "Thank you. Goodnight, Jonah."

"Goodnight, Savannah." Jonah was exhausted from the day's ride, but there was no way he would be finding sleep on this night, and it had nothing to do with the storm that raged.

*****

Broken pines and limbs lay everywhere. Jonah could tell the storm had taken its toll on the land, and from the looks of it, he couldn't see how the wagon stood strong. Perhaps it was the angels Savannah had prayed for the night before? But that was silly; how could angels exist?

Her sweet voice sang out from behind him. He loved hearing her sing to Rose as she fed her. It amazed him how good she was with his daughter.

Jonah yawned, feeling more tired than he had felt since they left Dahlonega. He hoped there were no more nights as last night was. He had not slept a wink.

Even if the storm was not raging, it would have been impossible to sleep with Savannah's soft body pressed up against him. She was only sixteen, but every bit a woman, and it pained him remembering his thoughts of the night before. Surely, if there was a God, He was not happy with him now.

CHAPTER 6

Days turned into weeks as Jonah and Savannah grew more accustomed to one another. Besides the incident with the rattlesnake and a couple of major storms, their journey had gone smoothly.

Was it just a matter of coincidence, or could it perhaps be the prayers he heard Savannah pray each morning and night, asking God for a safe journey?

Savannah consistently read from an old black Bible each evening, but Jonah still felt the words within the pages were nothing more than stories made up of fictional characters. To believe would be saying that a loving God had taken Clara away from him and their child, for no reason at all, and that was something he would never comprehend.

Jonah stopped the wagon on a small slope that overlooked large trees to the left and a valley of flat land to the right. A small stream ran between, dividing the trees from the prairie. How amazingly beautiful it was.

He had not seen another home anywhere for miles, and yet knew the closest town was approximately ten miles to the west of them, where they had stopped the day before for more supplies.

Could this be what he was looking for? Was this the place that Clara and he hoped to find to build their home and grow old in?

Nothing could possibly be more beautiful than the land he looked upon now. Arkansas was indeed a beautiful place, and he smiled, knowing how happy Clara would be if she were here with him now.

"Savannah," Jonah called out. She'd crawled in the back an hour before to feed Rose. "Yes, Jonah, is something wrong?"

"Are you finished feeding Rose?"

"Yes, she has gone back to sleep." Savannah stuck her head up through the opening of the wagon. "Wow, what a beautiful place."

"So, you like it, do you?"

"It's beautiful, yes. Are we in Arkansas?"

"Yes, we have been since the last village we went through."

"It's nothing like Georgia but still so beautiful."

"I think we have found our home. Do you think this place will do to build our cabin and barn? We could build our cabin over there," Jonah pointed to the place close to the stream. "And build a barn over there. There's plenty enough timber for both, and just look at all the great land for farming. And the closest village is only ten miles away, which could be traveled there and back in a day."

Savannah let her eyes slowly wander over the place once again, visualizing all that Jonah had said. Could it be true? Could their journey finally be over, and they were at last home?

"It's simply breathtaking," she clapped her hands, something she always did when she was excited. "This is a beautiful place to make a home. I shall love it all the days of my life."

"Then it's settled." Jonah pulled the brakes on the wagon and laid down the reins. "We are home, Savannah. At last, we are finally home."

*****

Within a week's time, Jonah had cut most of the trees he would use to build the cabin. Savannah loved his enthusiasm, as he explained to her how he would stack the logs and then place clay between the cracks, sealing out the wind of the harsh winter that was sure to come.

Savannah helped all she could, stacking the cuttings off the large trees that Jonah would not use on the cabin to be used in the wood stove that Jonah had brought along. The stove, invented by Benjamin Franklin in 1741, was one of Clara's favorite purchases after they had gotten married.

Savannah loved hearing the stories that Jonah told of Clara each night after she read several chapters of the Bible. It had not been easy at first for him to speak of his late wife, but now, after a little more than two months together, it was becoming easier.

Just hearing Jonah talk about her and the kind woman she was, Savannah could understand why he loved and missed her so much. Clara Bell had been a truly amazing, Christian woman.

"Would you like a cold drink?" Savannah asked Jonah, handing him a ladle of cold water she drew from the stream.

Jonah stopped and wiped the sweat from his brow and took what she offered. "Thank you. You have helped more than I ever thought you could, or would for that matter, and I thank you."

"It's my home too, Jonah, and it is my place to help all I can."

Jonah drank slowly, savoring the cold water, glad to have a stream nearby. "Well, I still thank you for everything. It has been a very long and tiring journey, and I am sure I was not the best company at times, yet still, you just keep smiling and doing all you can for me and *my* daughter." Jonah realized what he said and paused. "I mean *our* daughter. Please forgive me if I sometimes forget she is now your daughter also."

It felt great to hear Jonah speak those words. "Thank you, I appreciate your kindness. I am sorry Clara is no longer here, but I thank God daily that if anyone was to be your wife and Rose's mother other than Clara, it was me."

"But, Savannah….."

62

Savannah placed her finger over Jonah's mouth, feeling more comfortable with him now after all this time. "I know, you have told me one hundred times what I can expect, and I'm okay with that. I don't expect any more of you than you are ever willing to give when it comes to things of the heart."

He was realizing that more and more every day she owned a little more of his heart, and Clara was slowly slipping away. It pained him to see Clara fading and Savannah taking her place, but for the life of him, he couldn't stop it if he wanted to. "Well, I thank you." Jonah knew he need not say more.

She smiled, "You are quite welcome."

*****

"So, what do you think?" Jonah called out to her as she washed the nappies in the stream a few feet from the cabin.

"I think it's beautiful. Is it finished?"

"I just finished packing the last of the clay. We can move in."

Savannah got to her feet and clapped her hands. How wonderful it will be to get out of this wagon and in a house again. "That's wonderful! I'll start moving things inside just as soon as I have these hanging to dry."

"And I will have the wood stove working in no time, so you can cook inside instead of on an open fire."

"That would be great. Might even improve my cooking skills," she laughed.

"You cook great now, Savannah. I enjoy your cooking more than you realize."

Savannah nodded her thanks. Jonah was starting to brag on her more, and she welcomed it. Just the day before, he had told her she was beautiful. It had taken her by surprise, not knowing what to say in return, except a meek thank you.

"I'm looking forward to spring and planting vegetables to put up for winter. I'm glad you brought a few things that Clara had preserved; it will hold us over until the harvest comes in."

"I brought all I could. I wish I'd had room for more. I'm a pretty good hunter, so we should not go hungry."

"Yes, God has blessed us so much so far, and for that I am grateful." Savannah made it a priority to always give God the credit for everything they had. Jonah telling her he no longer believed only made her talk of God more in front of Him. She prayed daily that even if he never fell in love with her, that he would one day fall back in love with God and believe that He was just as real as always.

She hung the nappies on the line Jonah had placed between two trees and watched him carry in the wood stove.

Their house was finally finished and ready to make a home. The cabin was not as fancy as the house she grew up in, but she loved it even more, because it was theirs, a place to stay warm and dry, a place to cry and laugh and watch Rose grow into a woman as they would grow old themselves.

Oh Lord, if it be in thy will, please soften Jonah's heart even more toward me and help him to find a place there for me, so that he might love me like a wife needs to be loved. Help me also, Lord, to be the wife he needs me to be, his helpmate and friend as well as his lover if he needs that of me.

I so desire to be touched by him. Is this wrong of me, Lord?

*****

"Tomorrow I will start building you a bed, so you won't have to sleep on a bed roll any longer." Jonah finished the last piece of corn bread.

"I don't mind sleeping on a bed roll at all. You can build a bed later, if you want to start on the barn. The animals will need it in the winter weather."

"You are thoughtful, but I don't have time to build the kind of barn I want before the cold sets in. I plan to build a small shed that will be sufficient enough for winter, and I'll build a barn next spring. I also plan to get a couple of cattle to breed. Of course, I'll have to build a fence. There is so much for me to do that I'm not sure I'll get it done while I am still young enough to do it all," he laughed.

"You are strong and handsome, and you will get it all accomplished, I promise. I'll help all I can."

"I'm handsome, am I?" Jonah smiled, as he sipped his hot coffee.

Had she said that? It was a slip of the tongue. "Yes, of course you are," she said shyly, feeling her face turn warm.

"Well, thank you." Jonah ran his hand over the two days' stubble on his face. "I've never thought that of myself, but I thank you."

"Would you mind if I make curtains for the two windows out of the flour sacks?"

"Make anything you like—it is your home, too. You don't have to ask me."

Savannah chuckled. "That is not something I am accustomed to. My mother always asks my father's permission before doing anything."

"Yes, just knowing your father the short time I did, I can see that of him. Was he very strict with you and your siblings?"

"Yes, very. But I learned to adjust. I loved my father the best I could. I used to feel sorry for my mother."

"Was he not good to her?"

"He was good enough, I guess. But he was nothing like you and the gentle man that you are."

Jonah nodded and smiled. "Thank you. I hope I can be a good father, as well." Jonah looked toward Rose lying on the blanket, cooing up at the ceiling.

"Jonah, could I say something?"

"Sure." Jonah knew what was coming next and wasn't sure he was prepared to give an answer.

"I've been with you now for almost five months, and I have never seen you hold Rose. She is starting to make noises and flip over, and soon she will be talking and taking her first steps. You must hold her to bond with her."

Jonah closed his eyes and breathed in deeply before letting it out slowly. How could he tell Savannah the truth? What would she think of him then?

"Are you okay, Jonah? I've wanted to ask you a long time. I haven't pushed because you have been so busy. But now that the cabin is built and there will be time in the evenings, it would be a great time to get to know her."

"I do know her, Savannah; she is my daughter."

"This may be true, but she doesn't know *you*, Jonah. She hasn't been held by her father in a very long time."

Jonah got up from the chair he'd been sitting in and walked to the window to look out. He knew when he told her the truth, he would not be able to look her in the face. He hoped that the truth would not make her think less of him.

"Are you okay, Jonah? Nothing you say will turn me against you."

Had she read his thoughts? "I can't bear to hold her, Savannah."

"Why?" Savannah felt certain she knew the answer, but he needed to voice it. It would do him good to get it out.

"Because," he turned around with tears in his eyes and looked directly at Savannah.

"Because a part of me feels that she took Clara away from me!"

Savannah got to her feet and placed her arms around Jonah as he cried. She'd seen him with tears in his eyes but never sobbing as he was now.

Help him, Lord. Give him the peace that only You can.

"It's okay to feel those things," she said, softly. "It's okay to cry."

They stood in the middle of the floor for the longest, as the tears fell. At last the truth had come out, and Savannah hoped healing would take the place of what was once pain. Jonah pulled away and sat back down slowly. "You see, I'm not such a good person, after all."

She sat beside him and placed her hand on his. "You are wonderful, Jonah. It doesn't make me think any different. I know you love your daughter, and we will take it step by step, holding her a little longer each day. You will see, in time you will heal and realize that Rose had nothing to do with Clara's death. You will see how precious that little girl is, and she will grow to love you, just as I do."

"You love me?" Jonah asked in surprise.

"I do love you, Jonah. It's okay if you don't feel the same. I shall live forever with you thinking of me only as a friend."

Without second guessing, he pulled her close and pressed his lips to hers. The sweet taste of her was intoxicating, and as much as he wanted to pull away, he couldn't.

She welcomed the kiss and responded. Not until he heard her moan did he abruptly pull away.

"Oh no, what have I done?" Jonah took off out the door, even though it was almost dark outside. He wanted to leave, to think about what had just happened between them. Something he never intended to happen at all.

The last thing he wanted to do was change things now. It had been working so well the way it was, and he knew in his heart if he allowed himself to get too close, it could cost Savannah her life.

Savannah sat frozen for the longest time. There had been passion between them. Must he be feeling guilty?

Slowly walking to the window, she peered out. Where did he go?

Dear Lord, help him to see he did nothing wrong, that I am his wife.

As much as she hated the pain he must be feeling, she silently thanked God for allowing his heart to find hers, if only a very small portion.

*****

The next couple of weeks Jonah became very distant, and Savannah knew they had taken three steps backward instead of forward.

Jonah was staying longer outside in the evenings, working on the shed, and said few words only when spoken to.

Not only was he *not* holding his daughter, but he was avoiding her at all costs.

Savannah tasted the soup that she had prepared for dinner and set it on a makeshift table Jonah had made, promising to make a better one soon. She had called him in to eat earlier, and finally giving up, she started to feed Rose, who was now starting to eat solid soft foods.

The door opened and Jonah walked in, leaving his hat on the hook, as always.

Savannah jumped up to get his dinner, but Jonah motioned for her to stay seated. "Thank you, but go ahead and feed Rose; I am capable of serving my own dinner. You do too much for me."

She fed Rose another bite and took a bite herself. "That is my job, Jonah, and I don't mind to serve you."

"Nevertheless, I can do it." Jonah spooned out some of the hot soup in a bowl and took a piece of cornbread. "Looks and smells good, thank you."

"You're welcome."

Jonah sat down and started to eat. Like always since the kiss, the room grew deathly quiet. Savannah found the silence almost unbearable.

"Rose pulled up on her knees today. It won't be much longer before she is crawling and then walking."

"That's nice," Jonah said, and took another spoonful of hot soup.

"How is the shed coming?"

"Almost finished."

"The leaves are almost gone, and I can feel winter right around the corner."

"Yep."

She sighed. No matter how much she tried he would not carry on a conversation, but only respond to the questions asked. It was as if he was afraid to communicate because that might make him care more than he wanted to. To stay his distance meant never getting too close.

Jonah got up and placed his hat back on his head. "It was good, thank you. Don't wait up, I have work to do." And just like that, he was gone again.

Savannah stomped the floor. How could she ever get close to him if he would not even speak to her? And how would Rose know him if they never bonded? She was growing so fast, and Savannah was afraid he would miss the opportunity while she was still small. She had no answers. Oh, how she wished she could speak to her mother, who was always full of great advice.

That was it, she would write her mother a letter and have it ready to mail the next time Jonah rode into town.

Why had she not thought of that before now? She had promised her mother she would write when she arrived, and she had yet to accomplish that promise. She'd been so busy.

Of course, Jonah had not been back to the village since they arrived. With their supplies getting low, she knew it would be just a matter of time, and she would have the letter ready and waiting.

After getting Rose to sleep, she sat down at the table and started writing. She had so many things she needed to say.

Dear Mother,

I'm so sorry I haven't written to you before now. We arrived in Arkansas a little over two months ago and have been busy building a cabin. It is beautiful here and the cabin is small and quaint.

The journey to Arkansas was extremely long and hot, but we made it safely. I could feel your prayers and angels around us, protecting us through storms and snakes.

Jonah is now building a small shed to house the animals this winter. Next spring, he will build a barn and buy some cattle. The land here looks great for farming and planting vegetables. I am so grateful now that you taught me so much.

My cooking has much improved, and Jonah always tells me it's good. Of course, I know I will never be the cook that you are.

I have made curtains for our two windows out of flour sacks and tried to make the cabin look more like home.

I read from your Bible every night, even though Jonah says he no longer believes in God, since Clara died. I tell him I am reading to Rose the way you read to me, and I am, but I also know he must hear, just like you did with Father.

Even though it's been several months, Jonah still treats me as Rose's caregiver only. I thought I was making progress on capturing his heart until he kissed me and now has pulled away even further than before.

He never talks to me except to answer a question and the loneliness is almost more than I can bear.

I do so wish he could love me even if it was only half as much as he loved Clara. I need your advice Mother more than I ever have. I miss you terribly!

Please don't think I am upset about what I learned the morning Jonah picked me up about the trade father made for my hand in marriage. Where it was shocking at first, I feel it was in God's plan for my life.

I do so love being Rose's mother; she is such a delightful child and will be crawling soon. I plan to raise her, teaching her about God, just as you taught me. I know Clara would be proud that I read to her from God's Word each night.

Jonah said she was a good Christian woman and always prayed daily. I may never be as good a mother as Clara would have been, but I am going to do my very best.

I love being Jonah's wife also, even if there is no intimacy. He is the kindest, most gentle man.

I pray that someday he views me as a wife and not just a caregiver.

I cannot wait to hear from you. Please tell Father and Joseph and Mary I love them very much and miss them also.

Your daughter,
Savannah

CHAPTER 7

The air had been getting colder all day, and Jonah could tell by the clouds that snow was soon to come. He dreaded winter more so than ever. Being in the house so close to Savannah was not something he longed for.

For the past month he had avoided her, trying to keep a safe distance, not because he didn't trust her, but because he didn't trust himself.

When he kissed her, she stirred feelings that only Clara had been able to stir thus far. Savannah had no idea what she did to a man, and he was afraid that if he had not walked away, he would have carried it further than he ever intended to.

How could he do that to Clara when he had pledged to love no other for as long as he lived? Jonah closed the livestock in the small barn and closed the double doors when the first snowflake hit his face. The wind was picking up, and he was glad he had chosen to ride in to the village the day before to get supplies and carry Savannah's letter.

The deer roast she was cooking smelled wonderful as he entered the doorway and hung his hat. "It is starting to snow outside."

"Really?" Savannah said with excitement and hurried to the window to see.

"I'm not sure why you are excited. There's not much to do closed up in here all the time."

"Maybe you will be forced to talk to me more," she chuckled. "Dinner is ready. I'll get it on the table as quickly as I can."

"No rush." Jonah sat down and started taking off his heavy boots he'd had on since daybreak, ignoring Savannah's comment.

"Did the post office say how long it would take for the letter to be delivered?"

"No."

Savannah grumbled under her breath. No matter how much she tried there was just no communicating with Jonah, and it looked as if she might have to use drastic measures.

"You can come to the table now."

Jonah took a chair at the table, and Savannah spooned out a heaping of stew for Jonah with a biscuit and placed it in front of him. Then she picked up Rose and carried her to the table, and without asking, placed her in Jonah's lap.

"You can feed her tonight. Might as well learn how; she *is* your daughter."

Jonah froze as Savannah took a seat next to him. Never once since Rose's birth had he attempted to feed her; that had been Nelly's job and now Savannah's.

Savannah smiled. "You two look nice together. Just look at that sweet face looking up at her father. Let us pray." Savannah bowed her head. "Dear Father, we thank You for Your bountiful blessings You have given us. We thank You for this warm cabin and the food before us. You love us when we don't deserve to be loved, and You understand everything that is in our hearts. We ask You to lead us closer as a family and closer to You. In Jesus' name we pray. Amen."

Rose giggled, looking across at Savannah making a funny face. "Are you hungry, precious girl?"

Jonah let out the breath he'd been holding and took a small spoonful of stew before looking towards Savannah.

"Just put it to her mouth, she will know what to do with it. She will eat the broth from it. She's still too little to eat any of the meat."

Jonah did as he was instructed, and Rose eagerly took the spoon in her mouth. Over and over Jonah fed his daughter spoonful after spoonful. Savannah's heart burst with love as she saw Jonah's tension melt away.

"See how easy that is?" Savannah smiled at him. "You can eat at the same time, if you like."

"That's okay. I'll feed her first."

However you wish," Savannah commented, taking a bite of stew herself. "I hope you are not upset with me, Jonah, but I feel that Rose needs to know her father."

Jonah gave Rose another spoonful and looked toward Savannah before attempting to smile. "I'm not upset."

"Do you think it would be possible to get us a small tree to decorate for Christmas? My mother always asked my father to bring us one, and all us children would decorate it, making chains out of paper strips."

"I'll bring us in one."

"Thank you. And thank you for the yarn you brought me. It will make Rose a nice yarn doll. And the material is beautiful."

"You are welcome."

"Jonah, I wish it could go back to the way it was before the kiss, when you used to talk to me."

Jonah looked in her direction and then back to Rose. "It shouldn't have happened," he mumbled.

She grew quiet for a moment, praying silently about what to say next. "Jonah, we are out in the wilderness. There is no one anywhere that I can tell within at least ten miles. Winter is fast approaching, and Rose cannot yet communicate. I shall not keep my sanity if you only answer what is asked of you. Please, Jonah, talk to me the way you used to."

"I'm sorry; I will try to do better. You just don't understand."

"You are right; I don't understand how you felt when we kissed. I know your heart still belongs to Clara, and I imagine you felt guilt, but Jonah, as much as you wish she were here with you now, she isn't. You have nothing to feel guilty for. And distancing yourself from me all winter will only make things worse. As much as I don't understand how you felt, I do understand how it made *me* feel. There was passion between us. I felt it. Perhaps that is what upset you so. Perhaps you wish there had not been, but it was there just the same."

Jonah stood up and laid Rose on the blanket in front of the wood stove. "I think she is finished now."

"Here, I will dish you out more," Savannah offered.

"It's okay; I'm not very hungry anymore. I might eat later." Jonah walked over to the window to look out. So many thoughts running through his mind he wanted to scream. Yes, there had been passion between them, passion that should never have been there. How could he have allowed such a thing to happen?

Savannah knew she'd hit a nerve. This was not the time to keep on, but rather let it go. If there was one thing her mother had taught her, it was when to proceed forward and when to let it go, and this was that time.

*****

Savannah finished the yarn doll for Rose and hid it away for Christmas. She thanked God for the yarn Jonah had brought from the village and decided to make him a warm hat and scarf. It was easy to work on it without him knowing, since he was gone the biggest part of the day hunting and tending to the livestock.

Jonah was better with his communication since her talk, but there was still tension between them, and Savannah feared it may never be the same as it once was before the kiss.

The door opened and in came Jonah, carrying a spruce tree he had prepared with a base so it would stand. "Is this tree okay for you?"

Savannah got to her feet and clapped her hands with excitement. "It is beautiful—the best Christmas tree ever!"

"Where should I set it?"

"Over there," she pointed by the window. "Away from the stove so it doesn't dry out as quickly. Thank you so much, Jonah!"

"You are welcome. I want Rose to have a Christmas tree. Clara would have wanted that, too."

"I finished the yarn doll. Would you like to see it?"

"Sure." Jonah sat down to take off his boots next to the fire.

She pulled the doll out of her yarn basket and handed it to Jonah. "How do you like it?"

Jonah chuckled. "She will love it. Where did you learn to do that?"

"My mother taught me. My first doll was a yarn doll. I think she will like it. When she gets older, I will teach her how to make them also."

"Clara would be proud that you are going to teach her so much. Can you also teach her how to read?"

"Of course I can. I can teach you, too, if you are willing to learn."

"No need for it at my age."

"Well, of course there is. You could read God's Word if you knew how to read."

"You know how I feel about *God's Word*," he muttered, setting his boots aside.

"Well, you might feel differently if you could read it for yourself."

"I doubt that. It looks like another storm is coming toward us. We might get more snow." Jonah was best at changing the subject.

"I'll start working on the paper chains to place on the tree. Would you like to help me?"

"Sure, I guess."

Savannah hurried to get the materials on the table before Jonah changed his mind. It wasn't every day that she was able to work closely with him, and she welcomed it. She loved Rose, but she hungered for another adult to talk to.

Jonah came over and pulled out a chair under the table. "So how does this work?"

"It's easy. You just cut the paper in strips like this," she demonstrated. "And then glue the ends together using the glue I made. Then you place the next one inside the first."

"I'm sure Rose will love looking at the tree," he commented, doing as Savannah had instructed.

"Yes, I'm sure of it. Do you know what the tree symbolizes, Jonah?"

"I've never really thought about it."

"The cross. Jesus was nailed to a cross made from the wood of a tree. He died for us so that we may be saved. He took upon His back the stripes of our sins and made a way that we could go to heaven just by believing in Him. Christmas represents His birthday, and we give gifts because the wise men followed the star and gave our Savior gifts after His birth. They were wise and knew that He was the King of all Kings. He was the Son of God."

"That's a nice fairy tale."

Savannah reached over and placed her hand on top of Jonah's. "It's not a fairy tale, and you know it. You have never stopped believing in God, Jonah. You are just angry at Him and bitter. It's easier for you to think He doesn't exist than to try to understand why He took Clara home."

Jonah pulled back his hand and continued to cut the paper. "No loving God would have done that."

"No Jonah, you are wrong. Our earthly bodies don't last forever. God doesn't promise us tomorrow. I have no idea why He called Clara home at such a young age, right after your baby was born, but nevertheless, He did, and we are not to question that but have faith that she is with Him now. To not believe in Him is to not believe she is in heaven, and I know you don't believe that."

"If there *is* a heaven, she is there, I am certain."

Savannah nodded and shook her head. "You see—I knew you still believed in God."

Jonah chuckled. "If you say so." Jonah knew there was no use arguing with this beautiful woman. Yes, Rattle Box was the perfect nickname for her. Her father couldn't have come up with anything that fit her better.

*****

Savannah prepared the table with the turkey Jonah shot, the sweet potatoes he brought back from the village, and green beans she'd been saving that Clara had dried. She stood back and thanked God silently for the feast spread before her. It would be a wonderful Christmas indeed.

Jonah had been out in the shed since the early hours of morning, and she did pray he came in soon before the food grew cold. It was time for dinner over an hour past. What in the world must he be doing?

Rose cried out from the floor, and Savannah picked her up and gave her kisses on her cheek. "What are you crying for, sweet girl? Are you hungry?"

At last, the door opened and Jonah came in, dragging a bed covered in a light dusting of snow. "Merry Christmas," he said.

"Oh Jonah, you built a bed?"

"Let's just say I did the best I could with limited supplies. At least it will get you off the cold floor."

Savannah ran to him and hugged him tightly. Surprisingly to her, he did not pull away. "Thank you so much, Jonah, it is so beautiful. And the quilts Clara made will make it even more beautiful.

"Hang on, I will be right back." Jonah left again, and within minutes came back inside carrying another bed, a smaller version. "For Rose," he smiled.

Savannah laughed. "You are brilliant. It is also beautiful, but what about you?"

"I can sleep on the bed roll, as always. I'm used to it and don't mind."

"Jonah, the bed is plenty big enough for both of us. There is no harm in sleeping next to me."

Just as Jonah was about to explain why he wasn't ready for that, someone knocked on the door.

"Savannah, take Rose and go stand over there," Jonah pointed to the far end of the room, before picking up his gun.

"Who is it?" he asked, loudly.

"John Barge, ye neighbor, sir."

"We don't have any neighbors." Jonah knew better than to trust anyone.

"Not a close neighbor, sir. I live about fifteen miles east of you. I was coming back from the village and the weather started getting bad. I was wondering if perhaps I could stay in ye shed until morning. I promise to leave at first light."

"Jonah, open the door. It's the right thing to do," Savannah pleaded.

Jonah opened the door slowly, keeping his gun pointed at the unannounced stranger.

There before them stood an older gentleman of about seventy, shaking from the cold.

"I promise ye sir, I am completely harmless. May I just warm myself by ye fire?" Jonah looked past him into the darkness and saw an old wagon and a horse that looked as if it seen better days. "Take your horse to the shed for the night and come back. We were just about to eat dinner. You are welcome to join us."

"Thank ye so much, kind sir. I will be right back."

Jonah closed the door and looked toward Savannah. "You didn't mind that I asked him to stay for dinner, did you?"

"Of course not, Jonah, it's the Christian thing to do. He can sleep here on my bed roll, since you have made me this beautiful bed. Please don't make him stay in that cold shed. I'm afraid he might freeze to death at his age."

"Perhaps you are right, but I will not sleep a wink with a stranger in the house. And I'm going to take you up on your offer. We will all three sleep on the bed tonight, Rose between us. I will keep watch to make sure he is harmless."

Savannah smiled. "As you wish, Jonah. I will get an extra plate on the table."

*****

Savannah had never seen anyone who seemed so hungry and was grateful she had made such a feast.

"That sure was tasty, Mrs. Bell." John drank the last of his milk and wiped his mouth.

"Savannah is a good cook," Jonah smiled at her.

"Ye are a very lucky man to have such a beautiful wife and daughter. I once had a beautiful wife too, but the good Lord saw fit to carry her home before me. I'm afraid I'm not much of a cook, so forgive me if I seemed to enjoy myself more than I should."

"That's perfectly all right; we are glad you enjoyed it, right, Savannah?"

"That's right. We had no idea you lived so close. You should stop by more often."

"I did not realize anyone moved in until I went in to the village. I usually only go for supplies twice a year. I guess I should have gone before now. Martha always said I was a procrastinator," he chuckled.

"I'm just glad we were here. Not sure you would have made it fifteen miles in this weather," Jonah said.

"I tell ye, when I saw ye light, I thanked God for it. Ye being here saved my life and I am eternally grateful."

"Did you get enough to eat?" Savannah asked.

"Oh, yes, ma'am. I couldn't eat another bite."

"Not even a fried apple pie?"

"Well, maybe just one," he laughed.

*****

It was fun sitting around the stove hearing stories from John Barge. Jonah talked like never before, and Savannah enjoyed rocking Rose to sleep, listening to the two men compare tales of long ago.

Savannah was happy that never once did Jonah mention Clara. It was as if he wanted John to think that she was Rose's mother. After all, it wasn't a lie; she really *was* Rose's mother now, and there wasn't any place she'd rather be on this cold Christmas Eve night.

Savannah couldn't help but let her mind wander back to Christmases past, and she wondered what her family was doing.

She could see her mother sitting around the fireplace reading scriptures from a new Bible she managed to get from the mercantile.

Surely her mother wouldn't have gone long without the Word of God.

She hoped her mother wasn't terribly worried about her, for she had no idea how long it would take for a letter to get from Arkansas to Georgia and couldn't wait to hear back from her family.

Christmas had not gone as Savannah had planned, but it was nice just the same, and as she watched her husband talk to John, she smiled at how handsome he was.

She would just wait until tomorrow to give him his hat and scarf, which would be an even bigger surprise after Christmas was over.

Thank You, Jesus, for everything, and happy birthday to You!

CHAPTER 8

Winter hasn't been easy, but we have almost made it through. I stopped counting the snows long ago. Rose is crawling everywhere and pulling up. In just a matter of weeks she should be walking and I'm not sure we will be able to keep up with her.

Jonah has finally gotten tired of the cold floor and has started sleeping beside me on the bed, but of course he stays so close to the edge I'm always worried he will fall off. I am not sure if he will ever think of me as a wife, but at least he speaks to me. I think I shall go mad if he ever stops speaking to me again.

Jonah promised as soon as the snow melts, he will go to the village again and get more supplies. I hope that there is a letter waiting for me there from Mother. I can't imagine what they have been up to all these months.

Soon it will be our anniversary and it still amazes me that just a year ago I only loved Jonah from afar. Even after all this time there are days I still feel I love him from afar, for he will not allow me to get any closer.

So many nights I try to muster up the courage to slide next to him as he sleeps, but that would not be proper of me. So, I wait, night after night hoping that he will want me. My mother told me once they blocked their room with a blanket because a man had his needs. I am still puzzled over that one, because Jonah has none.

Or perhaps the guilt that he would be cheating on Clara still overwhelms him. At least he doesn't mention Clara as much as he used to, which is nice. Not that I mind, but it lets me know that perhaps he is finally able to let her go.

It's hard to believe it is already 1833, and Jonah says that we should expect many more settlers to come into the territory. I just hope they are kind. I for one can't wait to see what the future holds.

*****

"Jonah look," Savannah exclaimed, looking out the window.

"Don't tell me it's snowing again," he laughed.

"Of course not, just the opposite. The snow has all melted and the sun is shining. And listen, is that birds I hear singing?"

He loved her enthusiasm. She was so beautiful and had no idea of the depth of her beauty. "I guess this means you want me to travel to the village for supplies and check to see if you have a letter?"

"Oh yes, please, that would be lovely."

"Would you ladies like to bundle up and make the trip with me?"

"Oh, Jonah, could we, please? I would love that so very much!"

Jonah chuckled again. "Then get ready, and I shall hitch up the wagon."

Savannah quickly changed into her best dress.

She put the new dress on Rose that she had finished the day before and pulled her blonde hair up in a red ribbon. How cute she was.

It was the first time they had made the trip to the village with Jonah since they came to the valley, and Savannah was filled with excitement.

"Are you two ready?" Jonah asked, driving the wagon close to the door as Savannah came out holding Rose.

"We are ready, and very excited to be traveling in to the village."

He helped them onto the wagon's seat. "I'm sorry I didn't ask you the last couple of times I traveled for supplies. I am sure you want to get out of the house, too."

"It's okay. Thank you for thinking of us this time. The day is so beautiful for traveling."

"You both look lovely," Jonah commented.

"Thank you. I didn't want you to be ashamed of us," she giggled.

"Seriously, any man would be pleased to call you his wife. Giddy up," Jonah called out to the horses, sending them headed toward the village.

Savannah sat quietly, thinking about what he had said. He was proud to call her his wife? She would like nothing better than for him to *treat* her as his wife. She'd decided by mid-winter that she must get used to just being Jonah's friend and nothing more.

The ride to the village was beautiful, with spring coming alive all around them. There were so many things for Savannah to be excited about in her new life that she felt giddy from it all.

Jonah loved seeing the excitement on her face over simple things. So many others would have thought nothing of a ride in to town, but not her; she made note of everything and announced it, as a child would. She gave God credit for it all and thanked Him verbally.

It was hard for a man not to believe in God around Savannah. God meant everything to her and she spoke of Him often. Yet for Jonah, he had not felt God's presence since before Clara died, and even though he didn't try to discourage her, he knew it would not matter how he felt; she would not back down from her beliefs.

Jonah watched how his daughter interacted with her. Rose was now walking, and her blonde hair was the spitting image of her mother's, yet he knew she would always think of Savannah as such.

Rose adored Savannah and hung onto her constantly, and thanks to Savannah's stubbornness, he himself had formed a bond with her. It melted his heart when she called him Pa.

"Pa, Pa!" Rose screamed, pointing at a bird in the sky.

Savannah laughed, "She is more excited than I am."

"If that were possible," he chuckled.

"Oh, Jonah, we do so thank you for allowing us to make this journey with you."

"You would think riding across the wilderness for two months would make you tired of wagon travels for a while."

"I was glad when we made it to our home, this is true, but after being closed up all winter, I welcome the time to get out."

"What sort of supplies do we need?" Jonah asked. "I have enough skins here that we shall be able to get what is needed."

"Flour, sugar, meal, coffee and beans."

"The basics. What I meant is what do *you* need, as in personal things?"

"We could use more lye soap for washing clothes."

Jonah chuckled. "Do you need any material, yarn or paper? Rose loved her yarn doll; you could make another."

"She would like that, huh, Rose?" Rose was too busy looking around to pay attention to the conversation. "And if you want, you can pick out some material and I'll make you another shirt."

Jonah looked down at his shirt and back at Savannah. "Are you saying I need a new shirt?"

"It would be nice, yes."

"And what about you and Rose? Do you two need any material?"

"No, I'm good, and the flour sacks make such cute dresses for her, don't you think?"

Jonah looked down at Rose and agreed. Savannah had made her a beautiful dress and matching bow. "Yes, you do a good job sewing. Clara would be so grateful that you do so much for her; I know I am."

"She's a precious girl, and she learns so quickly."

"That's because of you, and all you have taught her." Jonah reached over and took her hand and squeezed it. "I am so very grateful."

Savannah's heart skipped a beat, she was almost certain. It was the first time Jonah had shown any sign of affection since the kiss that had kept him quiet for weeks.

"Thank you. I truly love this little girl."

"I know; it shows." Jonah turned loose of her hand and took the reins. "We are almost there. Would you mind if I get a haircut?"

"Of course not. Rose and I shall wait for you in the mercantile."

"Please stay inside where it's safe, and if anyone causes trouble for you, go to the front, close to the proprietor."

"Do you not think the village is safe?" Savannah was concerned, seeing the buildings coming onto the horizon.

"One can never be too careful. You are a beautiful woman. Any fool can see that."

Savannah suppressed her smile. She loved it when Jonah bragged on her.

"I'll be careful and keep a tight grip on Rose; don't worry."

"You can pick out the material you think would make me a great shirt," he joked, as the wagon pulled into the village. "Whoa," he yelled, pulling back on the reins and setting the brake.

"Wow, I feel a little out of place," Savannah said, in almost a whisper, referring to the lady walking out of the saloon with the low-cut dress and feather hat.

"Women like that are a dime a dozen; you are beautiful just the way you are." Jonah laid down the reins and jumped off the wagon. "Come here, pretty girl," he smiled at Rose and placed her on the ground. "You're next," he extended his hand to Savannah.

"Thank you so much. We will head toward the mercantile." She picked up Rose and started down the crowded boardwalk.

"Do you want me to walk you over?" he called.

"Of course not. Go get your hair cut, or I'll be making you matching bows like Rose."

Savannah felt as if she were in heaven. Never had she felt more like Jonah's wife and Rose's mother than she did today.

Jonah seemed to be feeling more comfortable around her, and she welcomed the change, even though the springtime had a way of making people happy. Perhaps he was finally getting used to the idea that she was his wife, and Clara wasn't coming back.

Savannah stayed on the boardwalk as she walked toward the mercantile. The music from the saloon played loudly as she was passing by, and Rose buried her face in her shoulder. She had never heard music before, and it frightened her. Savannah didn't slow down to look inside but hurried on to the mercantile.

*****

She loved Dolby's Mercantile. There was so much to choose from, unlike the one in Dahlonega or where they had stopped along the way to Arkansas. It was amazing, and Savannah stood for a moment to take it all in.

"Can I help you find something?" a plump woman asked.

"No, ma'am. I am waiting for my husband and want to look a bit, if I may?"

"Certainly, ma'am."

"Thank you." Savannah walked slowly over the wooden floor that shone like glass and held tightly to Rose who was pointing at everything she saw.

"Do you like that?" Savannah asked the toddler, who was reaching for a porcelain doll. "I used to have one similar, but I left it for Mary. Maybe someday your Pa can get you one, too. I'm afraid they are quite expensive. Let's go pick out some yarn for a new yarn doll, how about that?"

"Do you make yarn dolls, too?" a soft voice asked from behind her.

Savannah turned to see a red-haired girl who looked about her age, also carrying a small child.

"Yes, I do," Savannah answered. "My name is Savannah, and this is Rose, my daughter."

"I'm Amanda, but you can call me Mandy. This is my daughter, Rachel. She loves yarn dolls."

"So does Rose. So, where do you live?" Savannah was glad to have met someone of her own age. It had been a long time since she'd spoken with another female.

"We are just passing through. How about you?"

"About ten miles from here. It's quite a ride, but nothing like when we traveled from Georgia."

"I'm originally from Delaware, and yes, the ride is terrible. Lamar wanted to come for the farmland. He wants to travel a little further west."

"Where is Lamar now?"

"He's getting a haircut."

"So is Jonah; he gets one each time he comes to the village."

Mandy smiled. "Do your parents live in Georgia?"

"Yes, I miss my mother every day."

"I know what you mean. I had to leave my family, too."

"Mandy, are you ready to go?" a bearded man asked Mandy.

"Yes, I was just talking to Savannah. Savannah, this is my husband, Lamar."

Lamar held out his hand. "It's nice to meet you."

"It's nice to meet you both. Have a safe journey."

"Take care of yourself." Mandy smiled, and followed her husband out the door.

Savannah sighed, knowing she would probably never see her again. That was the downfall of living here—there were no neighbors close.

Savannah went close enough to the yarn to see which one Rose would pick, and she reached for a yellow bundle.

Savannah laughed, "A child after my own heart; that's my favorite color, too. Now let's pick out some material to make your pa a new shirt."

Jonah entered the mercantile and looked for Savannah.

He smiled when he spotted her, holding onto Rose and looking through the many bolts of material. It was easy to see her beauty. Any man would be a fool to not realize as much.

Her attitude on life was amazing, as she was able to find something good in any situation, so much like Clara, yet so different.

Could it be his heart was starting to melt a little more, and was it wrong to have feelings for someone other than Clara, the woman he'd pledged his heart to?

Most men would have already fallen for Savannah.

Savannah saw him watching her and smiled, motioning him her way. "How do you like this color? I think it would look great on you, and I think Rose agrees."

"Then it's settled; I'll get a new blue shirt. Have you two girls been having fun?"

"Yes, it's so good to be out, and the day is so beautiful. Just look at this place; it has everything!" she beamed.

Jonah laughed. "Yes, it does. Let me do some trading, and we shall be on our way to the post office."

"Oh yes, I can hardly wait!"

*****

"Aren't you going to open your letter?" Jonah asked on the way home.

Savannah held her letter as if it were her most prized possession. "Oh, I shall, I shall."

Jonah shook his head. "I shall never understand women."

She giggled. "I've been waiting all winter for this letter, and I want to read it at just the right moment."

"And when will the right time be?"

"Later tonight, after everything is finished, and Rose is sleeping."

"When you have alone time—makes perfect sense."

"See, it's not so hard to understand women," she smiled.

Savannah loved the warmth of spring and the birds that Rose was mesmerized with, but she couldn't wait for the day to draw to an end, so she could open the long-awaited letter to see how her family was faring.

*****

Savannah's patience amazed him. He watched her place the letter in her apron pocket, cook dinner, wash dishes, bathe Rose and get her to bed before finally sitting down in the rocking chair to pull out the letter.

"I'm going outside a bit and check on the animals. You need this time alone." Jonah left quietly, sure she'd not heard a word he'd spoken the past hour.

Savannah pulled the letter close to her nose and breathed in the fragrance, hoping she could smell her mother.

Trembling, she opened the letter slowly and pulled out the paper.

Dearest Savannah,
You have no idea how much it meant to receive your letter. I was beside myself with worry for you at least a month after I saw your wagon fade from my sight. But God reminded me that you were His daughter before you were mine and so I placed you in His hands.

Oh, sweet daughter, do not fear about Jonah's love for you. For as long as it has been since you wrote your letter to me, I am sure things are already better between you and Jonah, and if not, it is just a matter of time; for you are an angel and any man would love to have you as his own.

He is probably already in love with you, just afraid to voice it. He is probably showing his faithfulness to his late wife, which means he will show the same love to you. Patience is not always easy, but well worth it.

Be yourself sweet girl, and he will fall in love soon enough, and not be afraid to show you.

I'm so glad you are reading to Rose from my old Bible. The Bible says to train up a child in the way they should go and when they are older, they will not depart from it. You are a great mother; I always knew you would be.

And don't worry about Jonah not believing in God. He is still very bitter, but that too, shall pass in time.

I laughed when you said your cooking has much improved. I can remember when your father and I had just gotten married. I am amazed he stayed with me for it was not very good at all back then.

Speaking of your father, he is doing well.

Mary and Joseph are also good. I hate that Mary isn't old enough to remember you as the years go by, but Joseph misses you terribly. Perhaps you can also send him a letter along with the one you send me. I know he would like that. He can't understand why you got married and went away; breaks my heart really. Perhaps you can talk to him about it?

I'm so glad I taught you to sew. I am sure the curtains are beautiful. It's amazing what you can do with the material from flour sacks. I bet you are making Rose a lot of cute dresses also. She is lucky to have you as her mother.

I'm glad you feel that it was in God's plan for you to wed Jonah Bell. I am so very sorry I didn't tell you about the land trade. I wasn't sure how it would make you feel and felt bad enough as it was. I was against your father giving your hand in marriage without speaking to you about it. It just happened too quickly, and I am terribly sorry. Of course, from your letter you seem happy and that does my heart good to hear.

As far as me, I am good, but I miss you greatly. It just isn't the same since you left. Of course, now that I heard from you, I shall live in peace a little more.

I wish you the best my sweet daughter. Please take care of yourself and write back when you can. I love you,
Mother.

Savannah wiped a tear from her eye and placed the paper back inside the envelope. It would be several weeks before Jonah went back into town to carry another letter, and then even longer for her mother to send a reply. She knew she would read the letter repeatedly, to feel close to her mother. Oh, how her heart ached just to see her once again.

CHAPTER 9

John Barge arrived a little after daylight with the promise that he would more than willingly help Jonah build a barn and fence, in trade for the home-cooked meals Savannah would prepare while he stayed as a guest.

Jonah was sure it wouldn't take much longer than a couple of months with the help of John.

Even though John was much older than he, he was strong as an ox and willing to help, and Jonah welcomed the company of another man to talk to.

"These hotcakes are wonderful," John licked at his lips and drank the last of his coffee.

"You are much too kind," Savannah giggled. She loved to watch the way he enjoyed every bite of anything she set before him.

"Nah, you're just a great cook, ma'am."

"Don't you think it's about time you start calling me Savannah?"

"She's right, you know," Jonah agreed, "You are practically family."

John laughed. "Savannah it is, then. I wouldn't be here right now if it weren't for ye and Jonah's hospitality last Christmas. And the truth is, it was the best Christmas I'd had since Martha passed."

"Anytime John, our door is always open to you."

"How did ye manage to get a woman like Savannah?" John asked, winking at Jonah. Jonah watched the expression on Savannah's face change and knew she feared what his answer would be.

Jonah reached over the table and placed his hand on top of Savannah's. "I got lucky, John. I got darn lucky. And if we don't get started on that barn, it's going to take us forever to finish."

"I hear ye, Jonah, let's get to it."

Savannah watched the men go out the door and head toward the shed for the tools. Finally, it seemed that Jonah was acknowledging her as his wife, and she wondered why he never mentioned Clara in front of John. Surely John noticed that Rose looked nothing like her, or Jonah either, for that matter, but if he did, he never voiced it.

*****

After Savannah carried both the men some homemade buttered bread and milk for lunch, she hurried back to the cabin to write her mother and Joseph a letter. It had been on her mind the past week.

She smiled at Rose playing with the blocks that Jonah had made her for her birthday. She loved stacking them one by one, and laughing each time they came tumbling to the ground.

Dearest Mother,

I was so happy to receive your letter. So much so, that I am sure I have read it a dozen times or more. It makes me happy to feel close to you, knowing it was by your hand the words were formed.

I was never so grateful to see the snow melt and springtime finally arrive.

95

One of our neighbors, John Barge, is staying with us a couple of months to help Jonah build a barn and then a fence for the livestock Jonah wants to get.

John insists on sleeping in the shed, and I guess it's not so bad now that it is much warmer, and Jonah built him a cot to stay off the ground.

John says a couple needs their privacy, which is funny to me. He has no idea that Jonah and I live together as friends, not as husband and wife.

We have gotten much closer than the last time I wrote to you, and I can only pray that one day he might actually see me as someone he wants as a wife, not something he just says to people, but something he feels in his heart.

Rose is running everywhere and hard to keep up with. I just love being her mother and watching her grow up.

Isn't it funny how you can feel such a bond, and love a child so much that isn't actually yours?

I could only imagine what it would be like to have a child of my own. This is my biggest prayer mother, that one day Jonah would love me and want another child.

Fear plagues at me though because I feel that it might never be possible. Even if he could love me, bearing a child is what took his beloved Clara from him, and I am sure this is not something he would ever desire. I am starting to think maybe this is one of the reasons he doesn't desire to touch me in that way. Maybe it is starting to be fear more than guilt. In any case mother, please pray that God have His will in my life, whatever that may be.

Jonah says the next time he goes into the village he is going to bring back at least a dozen chickens that I am sure will soon turn into many more in the months to come. I am excited to have eggs to cook, and Jonah says the eggs are good for trading also.

He has plowed a large portion of our land and we have planted all kinds of vegetables to take to market and to put up for winter. I am excited because it keeps me busy. I not only can trade the extra eggs at market but I am going to try bringing some fried pies and some of my crochet also.

I am hoping by next Christmas we can afford to purchase a porcelain doll for Rose. I could just imagine her face when she sees it.

I do hope father and Joseph and Mary are doing well. I am also enclosing a letter for Joseph as you asked. Please assure him that I love him and miss him very much, just as I do the rest of you. Especially you mother. There are days I miss you so terribly, when I think of all the things I wish I could ask you. I love writing letters, but it takes so long in between.

Please know that I love you and miss you. Tell father I love him also.

Your daughter,
Savannah.

Writing her mother always made her sad; maybe because she knew that this was as close as she could possibly get.

Dear Joseph,
I hope you are doing well. I am sorry I will not be there for your birthday. Please know that I am thinking of you always and that I love you and miss you.

I am sorry that I did not explain to you that I was getting married and leaving.

You see, when people grow up and get married, they sometimes must move away to another place where farming is better.

*One day, Joseph, you too shall meet a woman that you
will fall in love with and have a home of your own.*

*Maybe someday when you become a man you can travel
to Arkansas to see me. I would like that very much.*

*Until then, I will make sure I write you letters each time
I write mother. I am sorry that I did not write to you last
time, please forgive me.*

*Arkansas is beautiful. It's not mountains like Dahlonega
but still beautiful.*

*We live in a cabin that Jonah built and now he is building
a barn for the livestock. It won't be as big as the one you have
back home, but it will be big enough to house several horses
and cattle and hold the hay for the winter.*

*I do hope you are doing good in school, you were always
such a smart boy.*

I love you, Joseph, very much.

*Please do not be upset with me for leaving the way I
did. I will pray for you daily and I hope you pray for me
also.*

*Please be a great big brother to your sister and teach her
all the things you know.*

I hope you have a wonderful birthday.

I love you always,

Savannah.

*****

"I sure wish I'd known you when I built the cabin last fall,"
Jonah said to John, wiping the sweat that beaded on his forehead,
as the last of the timber they would need fell.

"And I am glad ye built the cabin, or my bones would probably
still be somewhere on this property," John laughed.

Jonah chuckled with him. He liked John. He reminded him of his father who passed away when he was just a young boy. "If you need work around your house when this is finished, it would do me good to ride over and lend a hand. My pleasure, for sure."

"Mind if we sit a spell?" John asked, sitting down on a fallen tree stump. "I reckon my body isn't as young as it used to be."

Jonah took a seat beside him and looked toward the cabin at the smoke billowing from the chimney. "Savannah must be starting dinner. She's making us rabbit stew and cornbread."

"Sounds tasty. I sure miss my Martha's cooking. I thank ye for allowing me to sit at your table and feast with ye."

Jonah laughed aloud. "How else would I pay you for all you have done to lend a hand?"

"Oh, I love helping out. I was referring to the night you took in a perfect stranger out of the cold and fed him well."

"That's what neighbors do; it's called hospitality."

John chuckled, remembering. "Yes sir, ye held that rifle so tight aimed straight for my heart."

Jonah laughed. "One cannot be too careful out here with no one around for miles."

"Oh, I don't blame ye. I must have looked a sight—half frozen solid, I was."

"Forgive me."

"I'd have acted the same if I had a wife and small child to protect. Think nothing of it; there is nothing to forgive."

"I am hoping, if weather permits, we have a nice crop this year. Savanah plans to put up all the food she can for the winter, and I know there will be enough to share."

"Ye are both much too kind to me. I do appreciate it. What a lucky man ye are to have a wife as beautiful and caring as Savannah. My Martha was the same. She would have handed ye the shirt off her back if she thought it would help another soul."

"Yes, Savannah is wonderful. I am a lucky man to have her as a wife."

"Ye are young enough to be my son, Jonah, and I feel we have grown close enough to speak freely, am I right?"

It was easy to see something weighed heavy on John's heart. "Yes, please speak freely."

"In the time I have had the pleasure of being in the company of such a fine couple, I cannot help but to sense that something is wrong. I have not been able to pinpoint it, but there is a distance between ye two that I am concerned about."

"A distance?" Jonah knew what he meant. Of course, there was a distance.

"Yes, a distance. I don't see it coming from Savannah, but from ye, son."

"You mean I act as though I don't love my family?"

"Oh no, son, I can see a plenty that ye love Savannah and Rose more than ye own life.

What I mean is that I see a distance, like ye are afraid to show it."

"You mean with Savannah or with Rose?"

"Both actually."

"I guess I have a lot to learn in the love department, John."

"I am not young anymore, Jonah, and I never knew that much about love myself in my younger years, but I know I never missed a day without telling Martha how much she meant to me. I hurt every day of my life that she's been gone from this world. The only thing that keeps me going is knowing she is with Jesus, and one day I will see her again."

Jonah thought back over the past year of knowing Savannah. Never once had he told her he loved her; Rose either, for that matter. But why would he tell Savannah that, if he still loved Clara? And Rose was so young, how could she possibly know what love is?

"I am sorry if I have brought up a sore subject; I shall learn to keep my opinions to myself. Martha always said it was a weakness of mine, to dish out opinions."

"It's okay, John, I value your opinion and appreciate having someone to talk to about things. Can I tell you something, John?" Jonah thought it was time to tell him what was going on, so he would understand why there was a distance to begin with.

"Ye can tell me anything and it will stay right here, between us."

"Savannah is not Rose's real mother. My first wife, Clara, died the night Rose was born."

John chewed a long strand of grass and studied Jonah for a moment. "I see."

"I only married Savannah to come across the country with Rose and I, to take care of her as I traveled. I thought it was the proper thing to do under the circumstances."

"But yet ye love Savannah with all ye heart, any fool can see that."

Jonah looked back toward the cabin once again and grew silent. Was his heart starting to belong to her after all this time? Was Clara slipping away?

"It's easy to see ye love her, Jonah. Maybe ye didn't set out to love her, but ye do just the same."

"It's hard, John. It's hard when I pledged my heart to Clara. I loved Clara more than life itself."

John nodded his head in agreement. "And ye don't feel that ye should love Savannah as much, and yet ye do, and so ye pull back because the thought of it terrifies ye. Is that true?"

Jonah took a deep breath and let it out slowly. Maybe John was right. He was scared to let his heart ever love as deeply as he had loved Clara. "Maybe you are right."

"It's okay to love Savannah; she is a good woman and deserves ye love."

"She deserves more than my love. She deserves more than I could ever give her."

"Savannah seems happy and content, and she adores ye and Rose."

Jonah smiled. "Yes, Rose is special, just like her mother was; anyone would adore her."

"What do ye think Savannah deserves that ye cannot give her?" John spread out his arms, looking towards the farm in front of him.

"A man that could fully love her and give her children of her own. A man that isn't still in love with a ghost, a memory that he pledged his love to and promised to never let another come between them."

"I remember those vows well, Jonah," John quickly stated. "I do believe they went something like, till *death* do us part."

Jonah looked at him a moment. Oh, how he hated that word. "But even death cannot stop me from loving Clara."

"This I understand, but death breaks the pledge and allows ye to love another. Ye are a young man, Jonah, with so much of life still left to live. Ye can always love ye first wife, and still have enough love for Savannah. If ye think ye are happy now, just imagine how much happier ye would be if ye let that love show."

"But you don't understand. It goes much deeper than that. Things are good between Savannah and I, and I would like to keep them the way they are. Getting closer would only complicate things."

"Ye are afraid to get close. Ye are afraid Savannah will get with child."

There, he said it. Jonah knew that was the reason he pulled away each time he felt himself being drawn to her.

That was the reason he ran from her after the kiss, when deep within him she stirred the feelings that only Clara had been able to awaken before that.

Maybe all this time he didn't blame Rose at all, but himself. Because of his own selfish needs, Clara had died.

Jonah buried his face in his hands. When would the pain end? Maybe there is no end.

John moved close and put his hand on Jonah's shoulder. "It's okay, son. It was no one's fault ye first wife went to be with Jesus. We all have a time and season on this earth."

"I'm so angry with God. Clara was a good person. She did not deserve to die."

"*Who* deserves to die?" John shrugged. "Life and death are all a part of God's plan for us. We all fall short of the glory of God, yet He loves us the same. I did not like losing Martha either, but for some reason God called her home before me. Maybe it was to help ye build this here barn," John managed to smile.

"Do you really believe in God, John, even after losing Martha?"

"Why, most certainly. Maybe more so now than ever."

"How do you mean?"

"I know Martha is with Jesus, because Martha loved Him with all her heart, mind and soul. And God's Word says to be without body is to be in His presence. Martha had suffered through a terrible illness, and the night I held her hand and watch her breathe her last breath I knew her pain was finally over. It would have been selfish of me to have wanted her to stay and suffer."

"Yet if God is real, He could have healed her and taken away her pain."

John smiled. "Yes, God has that power. But only God sees the big picture. Maybe taking her to be with Him *was* healing her."

"If there *is* a God, I will *never* understand Him."

John chuckled. "It is not for us to understand, but to have faith in Him. Clara is with Jesus, and that alone should give ye comfort and peace. Maybe this was in God's plan, for ye to be with Savannah and have more babies and live here in Arkansas Territory, and raise a barn with this old man named John."

Jonah managed a smile and shook his head. "Savannah wants me to believe in God again."

"I don't see that ye ever did stop believing; ye just grew bitter. God understands all that. It's okay to talk to Him about it."

"Thank you for speaking with your heart. I appreciate you letting me tell you that."

"Anytime, son. Now, we have a barn to bring to life, and sitting here isn't going to get us any closer to dinner," John laughed.

CHAPTER 10

Savannah loved watching Rose play in the creek as Jonah and John finished up the last of the fence posts.

Their home had grown into a beautiful place that to Savannah was truly a paradise. Savannah planned to make his favorite dish for dinner and send him home tomorrow with plenty of fresh, dried, and pickled goods from their garden.

God had blessed them well and sent enough rain that the crops were bountiful.

As much as Savannah had grown to love John, she was eager for him to be on his way and have alone time with Jonah once again.

He had gotten better at showing he cared, but there was still a great distance between them, and she felt certain that it was just a matter of time now before things would be as they should be, or at least she prayed daily that they soon would be.

"Water cold, Momma."

Savannah smiled at the beautiful blonde who waded knee-deep, playing with a wooden bowl from the kitchen that Jonah made.

"Yes, it's cold," Savannah laughed. Rose wasn't quite two yet and her vocabulary amazed her.

Savannah leaned back against the tree trunk and started writing the words that had kept coming into her head since daybreak.

A river runs over it, and a river runs through it.
And my father had traded me for it.
Now hope lends its ear to me, one day at a time.
Guided by the land and by His hand.
Maybe one day, he will be mine.
For the one-hundred acres wasn't just land,
It was a promise to me, the love he needed.
Jonah worked the land hard, far and wide,
With me always by his side.
Spring has sprung, and the work had to be done,
And in your eyes, I see your love has begun.
It grows slowly like fruit on a vine.
Our beautiful place one day will be,
A true home for you and me.
Rose is blonde, the sky is blue,
And oh, how we both love you!

*****

"That was the most amazing meal, Savannah. I will miss ye cooking," John leaned back in his chair and rubbed his belly. Even though he worked hard daily, he was certain he had gained a few pounds over the last several months.

It was now mid-summer, as Jonah had decided to slow down with the building and take their time. He valued his friend's health and did not wish to push him.

"I am glad you liked it, but I am sure you are ready to get back to your home," she smiled.

"Since I have been here, I was not able to plant a field of crops myself, so I appreciate ye sharing ye blessings with me. And I appreciate ye letting me bring over my cow and horse to tend while I was here," he added, looking toward Jonah.

"Don't mention it, John. The barn was much bigger than the cabin, and it would have been impossible alone. Is there anything you need me to come and help you with on your own farm?"

"No, I am not even sure I would call it a farm anymore. Since Martha died, I have let things go a great deal. Didn't have the heart right at first, and now I have grown used to it. Besides, one man doesn't need much."

"Well, my offer is there should you ever need me."

"Pa, look!" Rose pointed towards the windowsill. A cardinal had perched himself near the glass in full view.

"How beautiful," Savannah exclaimed.

"It is said that when one sees a red bird, we are to make a wish," John said. "I used to have lots of wishes when I was younger, but now I am just grateful to wake up each morning."

Savannah picked up Rose and moved slowly toward the window without scaring off the red bird. "Isn't it a beautiful bird, Rose?"

"Beau-ti-ful," Rose piped.

John stood up from the table and stretched. "Don't worry about making me breakfast in the morning; I will leave at first light without waking ye. I think I will turn in early tonight and get some rest. Thank ye both again for all ye hospitality ye have shown this old man."

Savannah set Rose down and hugged him tight. "I love you, John Barge, and I hope you do come back to visit us soon."

"I love ye too, Savannah, all three of ye," he patted Rose on top of the head.

Jonah extended his hand and decided to hug him instead. They had gotten much too close for a simple handshake. "Thank you, John, there's no way I could have done it without you."

"Anytime, Jonah, anytime at all." John left the house abruptly, his eyes filled with tears.

"Why do you suppose he left like that? He always hangs around way after dinner and listens to me read from the Bible," Savannah was confused.

"I'm not quite sure. Perhaps he feels that he has wore out his welcome."

"That is just plain silly; he knows better than that. Perhaps you need to go check on him, Jonah, and ask him. It isn't even dark yet."

"Perhaps you are right. I will go." Jonah put on his hat and left to go find John.

"Men are so confusing sometimes, Rose," Savannah smiled, picking her up once again and hugging her tight. "I do so love you, Rose."

*****

Jonah entered the shed to find John placing his clothes into his bag. "Is everything okay, John?"

John wiped at a tear and smiled. "Yes, of course, why do you ask?"

"Because you have been with us now several months and you have never left like that. You always stay and play with Rose and listen to Savannah read from the Bible. Are you feeling all right?"

John sat down on the cot that Jonah made for him and sighed. "It isn't easy leaving, going back to that empty house. The loneliness can sometimes get to a man."

"Then why are you in such a hurry?"

"Because, Jonah, as much as I would like to feel like part of the family, ye family is that woman and little girl in there. Ye need alone time with ye family now, Jonah. I have taken ye away for months and come between ye."

"Don't be silly; that is preposterous."

"Jonah, Savannah needs ye. Rose needs ye. Ye need quality time with ye family, Jonah. I will miss ye all terribly, but I will be all right. I will stop in to visit ye each time I am traveling to get supplies."

"You know, you don't have to go. We can build a small cabin for you right here on this property, so you can be close to us. There is no reason for you to be alone."

John stood and smiled. "Ye know I have grown to love ye like a son, and I do believe ye meant what ye just said, but I cannot do that, Jonah. I have had my time, my wife and my farm. God never seen fit to bless us with children, but I like to say if He had, my child would be just like you."

"Then why leave? Just stay here with us."

John smiled again. "I am much older than ye, Jonah, and my time on this earth is limited. Ye need this time with ye wife and daughter. Have no worries. I promise to stop in from time to time. I love ye, Jonah." John hugged him again.

"I love you too, John. Thank you. There are no words to thank you enough."

*****

The village was busy with travelers on this hot summer day. Savannah was excited to have another letter from her mother and just as before had stuck it into her pocket to save for later.

Instead of trading even for the supplies they needed, the proprietor not only gave them what they needed, but handed Jonah cash as well, for the beans, tomatoes, corn and pickles Savannah had brought along with them. He also paid well for the crocheted items she had been working on and the fried pies she had made fresh that morning.

Never had she felt as rich as she did today. It was the first time she'd been paid for anything she worked for.

Jonah left them to go to the barber shop for a haircut, and Savannah carried Rose down the boardwalk towards the wagon.

As she walked by the saloon, the lady wearing the tight dress walked out. "Hello there," she called from behind her.

Savannah turned to see her smiling down at her shoes that were streaked in mud from the rain the day before. "Yes, hello, how are you?" Savannah refused to not be polite even though this woman got under her skin the way she smirked at her. Why must there be one in every village?

"I am great. So where is that fine husband of yours?" she asked, looking to the street beyond.

"He is getting a haircut. If you will excuse me," Savannah took Rose tighter by the hand and started again for the wagon. Maybe she should have waited inside the mercantile a bit longer.

"Why do you run off?" the woman yelled, hurrying to catch up.

"And why must you follow me? Surely there is nothing you need from me. You seem to have everything you need."

"Forgive me if I have come off as being rude. I find you very beautiful. I just wanted to say hello and be a friend."

Savannah scoffed. "Beautiful? You have all but thrown insults at me by your tone and the way you look at me as if I cannot get a husband that is handsome."

The lady giggled. "Forgive me, again. I must learn to keep my facial expressions to myself. I was wondering if perhaps you would like some clothes I no longer wear."

"Clothes?" Savannah looked her over with her low-cut dress that fit so tight she wondered how she could breathe comfortably. "Are you serious?"

"Of course I am. We look to be about the same size, and I have plenty."

"Excuse me for saying this, but I live on a farm and not the village hotel. I am afraid your kind of clothing would not be appropriate for tending the fields and picking vegetables in."

"Maybe so, but it might spark up things with that handsome husband of yours."

"Does it look like we need more sparks than we already have?" Savannah was growing furious.

"Listen honey, I am only trying to help. You got what it takes, Sugar, you just need to flaunt it a little."

"I thank you for your offer, but no thank you. Have a good day." Savannah took off for the wagon without looking back. How dare she offer to give her some of her devil's clothing? Her father would kill her if he ever saw her in anything such as that.

She placed Rose in the back of the wagon to play with her blocks and watched Jonah walking toward them. He truly was the most handsome man the village had seen, and she felt proud to call him her husband.

"I really wish you girls would wait for me to come find you in the store and stay off the streets until I am with you," he said as he climbed on the wagon seat.

"I am sorry; I thought we would save more time if you did not have to come in search of us. Do you really feel it is dangerous here?"

"There's a lot of travelers coming through this time of year, and one can never be too sure. It's better to be safe than sorry. Giddy up," Jonah called out, setting the horses trotting off in the direction to pick up the dozen chickens.

"I am excited about the chickens, Jonah. I know Rose and I will name each one."

He laughed. "I wouldn't get too attached. As time goes on, there will be chicks and too many roosters, and fried chicken sounds mighty good to me."

"Maybe so as time goes on, but for the first dozen they will become family and they deserve names."

He chuckled again. Savannah amazed him more every day. He had done right by choosing her to be his wife. Rose adored her and thought of her as a mother, and he knew that each day his heart melted a little more.

*****

Savannah had been unusually quiet on the ride home. Her mind kept going back to what the lady from the saloon said to her.

Maybe Jonah would love her more if she *flaunted* it, as she called it. But then that would not be proper; or would it? After all, he was her husband.

"I have never seen you so quiet," Jonah said, as he helped her from the wagon when they arrived home.

"I'm sorry, I was just listening to the chickens clucking. I am excited to have them. It will be fun gathering eggs and having them to cook with."

"Savannah, I must say, it does not take much to excite you. I have never seen anyone so excited over chickens before," Jonah laughed.

"You will be excited, too, when my cooking much improves because of the eggs."

"And as I have said before, you are a great cook, even now."

"Can I ask you a question?" Savannah had been thinking about it all the way home. And as they entered the house, she couldn't wait any longer.

"Should I be worried?"

"Whatever do you mean?

"Well," Jonah stated, "each time you start a question by asking if you can ask one, it is usually a hard question to answer."

"It is something I have wanted to ask and never did, because I was afraid of the answer, but I am not afraid any longer. I think I can handle your answer now."

Jonah looked at her in question, "Go ahead. I feel as if I do not have a choice. I will answer the best I can."

"Was Clara beautiful?"

"Yes, but you know that. You have seen Clara."

"Yes, to me she was beautiful, but was she beautiful to you?"

Jonah rubbed his clean-shaven face. "That is a strange question. I married her, so of course I thought she was beautiful."

"Jonah, many men are married to women that are not beautiful."

"Maybe not to you, but to them, I am sure they are."

"Do you think?" Savannah had never thought of it that way. Perhaps they were. Perhaps love made you see beauty even if there wasn't any real beauty.

"Why did you ask that?" Jonah was still confused.

"Do you think I am beautiful?"

Jonah grinned, slowly. So, *this* was the *real* question. "Yes, Savannah. You are beautiful."

"But in a different way than Clara was beautiful, right?"

"What do you mean?"

"I mean you think I am beautiful, but not like Clara was beautiful?"

"I never said that, you did. You, my dear Savannah, are putting words in my mouth."

Savannah sighed and sat down in a kitchen chair. "Is it because I am so much younger than you, and you see me as a child and not a woman?"

Jonah took a seat beside her, knowing that whatever he said could and would be used against him. This was something he intended to approach delicately. "No, Savannah, I do not see you as a child at all."

"So, our age difference doesn't bother you?"

"Does it bother you?" Jonah turned the question back to her.

"Of course, it doesn't."

"Then why should it bother me?"

"But Clara was more your age."

Jonah reached across and took her hand, so small in his. "And your point is what, Savannah?"

"That I am not as beautiful and too young for you to ever love me the way you loved Clara." Savannah started to cry, not wanting to.

"Oh Savannah, that is not it at all, and you know this."

"Then why can you not love *me*, Jonah? What am I doing wrong? What am I not doing right?"

"You do nothing wrong. You do everything right. It is not you, Savannah; it is I who has the problem."

"What's the problem then? I mean, tell me, Jonah; I can take it. I am almost eighteen now and old enough to know the truth. I mean, at first I thought it was because you just could not get over the grief of losing her, and after all this time, I see that your heart may never mend. Each time I hope we might be getting close, you push me further back."

"How have I pushed you back, Savannah? I thought I had been doing much better."

"I don't mean push me back literally. I mean you won't allow yourself to get close. You sleep so far on the edge of the bed, it's like you hang on for dear life!!"

Jonah chuckled at that statement. "I don't want to crowd you."

"Crowd me? Jonah, I long for you to just touch me, even if it is merely your toe on my leg."

"Oh, Savannah," Jonah smiled. "Please be patient with me. I did not bring you into this marriage without telling you how I felt. I told you from day one what to expect."

"Yes, that you did, and I understood that almost two years ago, but I prayed time would heal your broken heart, and I might find myself the wife of a husband that actually desired me, even just a little bit."

"Sweet Savannah," he wiped a tear from her eye. "It is not that I do not desire you at all."

"Then what, Jonah?"

"I am a messed-up man, Savannah. Please, I will ask you again to be patient with me." Jonah kissed her on the forehead and went to get his hat. "Please don't think I am running from this conversation. I need to go unhitch the team." And just like that, he was gone.

Savannah wiped the tears and watched Rose play beside her.

It was true, he had told her from the very beginning what to expect. Why could she not let it go and be happy the way things were?

She wanted to be loved, the way a woman desired to be loved, to be held and make love. She wanted to feel his lips on hers again, and felt that she would never be able to. She wanted to have children of her own and watch them grow up as Rose's sister or brother.

Was it so wrong to want these things?

Savannah reached in her pocket and pulled out her mother's letter. Maybe this was a good time.

Dearest Savannah,

Joseph was thrilled to get your letter. He has read it over and over since he received it. Now he says when he is a man, he will ride his horse to visit you. It is good to see him with a dream.

Mary is starting to read basic words. She is doing good also. She loves the doll you left her. It was so sweet of you to do that, for I know how much it always meant to you.

Your father is still like always, working on the farm and enjoying his evenings on the porch with his lemonade. It has been the most beautiful summer, but I am afraid fall is fast approaching.

It still doesn't feel like it has been almost two years since I last saw you. I am sure you are still reading from my Bible each night. Don't ever stop. I know it is just a matter of time that Jonah believes again, if he hasn't started back already.

I have been doing a lot of sewing for the town folk. It is enough to keep me busy on top of everything else. But I do so enjoy sewing, you always knew that.

How did your crops turn out? Was it a good harvest? I bet you have put up many things to have for winter. I have been working at that myself. I miss you here to help me. I never realized all you did until you were no longer here. You were always such a good helpful daughter.

Miss Blue, your favorite cow had two babies at one time. Mary and Joseph named them Jonah and Savannah. Joseph said it helps him remember you.

How are you and Jonah doing? I know he is deeply in love with you by now. If he hasn't told you, just be patient. Sometimes it takes hearts longer to mend than others.

There is not a man alive that couldn't love you if they got to know you. You are truly one of a kind.

Hang in there, beautiful girl, you are a wonderful wife and mother and it is time you start seeing yourself as such.

I love you so very much and miss you more than you know,
Love, Mother.

Savannah folded the letter and placed it in the back of her Bible with the other. At least she had some form of communication with her family, even if they were so many miles apart.

It was time to put her thoughts behind her and start dinner. Her family would be hungry, and it would be dark soon enough.

CHAPTER 11

The first snow was starting to fall as Jonah cut down the tree to bring home to decorate for Christmas. It seemed as if it were just yesterday he'd brought their first tree into their new home.

He hoisted the tree into the bed of the wagon and started back toward their cabin. Darkness approached much earlier this time of year, and he couldn't help but think of John and the night they'd first met a year ago.

The cabin looked warm as he came into the valley with the smoke coming from the chimney. The light that glowed from inside was welcoming, and he knew Savannah was preparing their dinner.

He imagined Rose would be sitting on the floor playing with her blocks and yarn dolls.

This was his life now. Not back in Georgia with Clara as they awaited their baby, but here in Arkansas, with his and Clara's child, and Savannah, who tried so hard to be a good wife to him and mother to Rose.

He sometimes wished he'd married an older widowed lady, who could have taken care of his daughter and asked nothing of him in return, except a home. A home he could supply.

Nothing had been fair to Savannah. Life had dealt her a bad hand.

Forced to marry a man she didn't love and to become a mother to a child she didn't know. To be rooted up with two days' notice and moved miles away from the only home she knew, possibly to never to see her family again.

How was any of that fair? Yet day after day, Savannah did all she could to make their house a home and never complain.

All she asked for was love, and love the way she desired it from him was something he was almost certain he may never be able to give.

Jonah stopped the wagon a few feet from the house and looked in the window. Savannah danced around singing songs to Rose, as Rose laughed and clapped her hands for more. Oh, how he wanted to sweep Savannah up in his arms the way he used to do Clara and shower her with kisses until she laughed.

Lately he had been having dreams about Clara, and before he could wake, it turned into Savannah. In his dreams, it felt right and wonderful, but when he awoke, he still felt the pain of guilt.

He thought a lot about what John had told him that day, and that he shouldn't feel guilty. Maybe it *was* time to move on, but how? Where would he begin after all this time? He'd been sleeping with Savannah for months now, but other than the night in the wagon with the storm raging outside, he'd never once allowed their bodies to touch.

Oh, Clara, what would you think of me desiring another woman?

Would it upset you, or would you give me your blessing, knowing you are never coming back?

Are you upset that I still feel anger toward God?

Would you have felt the same if it had been me that left you alone with Rose? But of course, you would not have, for you loved God with everything you had and would have trusted that it would have been His will.

So why, Clara, why am I still so bitter? Why can't I let you go? Why, after all this time, does it still feel so badly inside?

The snow was picking up, and the wind was starting to howl. Jonah could feel that a blizzard was on its way, and he dreaded being closed so closely in the cabin.

Winters in Arkansas could sometimes be harsh. A man could get lost out in a blizzard, and he was grateful they had prepared their food supply.

He climbed down from the wagon seat to unhitch the team. Might as well get used to life as it was, because he had no idea how to make things better.

*****

The tree is beautiful, Jonah. I do believe that it is even better than last year's tree. Thank you for choosing one so beautiful to grace our home.

"Would you like me to help with the decorations this year?" Jonah asked, sitting down at the table where the paper and glue were waiting.

"Yes, that would be just lovely, thank you."

Jonah loved her childlike enthusiasm. The simplest things excited her. He loved the way she glowed and found excitement in life, even though he knew she was hurting inside. "There is something I want to talk to you about," Jonah said, reaching for a piece of paper strip and glue.

"What is that?"

"What would you think of building a cabin half this size in the spring, close to this one?"

Savannah studied Jonah's face, trying to follow his thoughts. "I am confused. Please don't tell me you wish to sleep in another house, away from Rose and me."

Jonah chuckled. "I never thought of that, not even once. No, I was thinking of moving John Barge here, to live beside us, so he wouldn't be alone."

Savannah smiled that huge smile Jonah loved. "You do love him, don't you, Jonah?"

"He is like a father to me, and I can't forget what he said to me the night before he left. I have never seen him so heartbroken."

"I thought you asked him to stay, and he would not."

"I did, but only because he thought you and I needed time alone. Besides, who would want to live in the shed with the livestock? I imagine if I built a nice little cabin and went to fetch him, he would come."

"You are a good man, Jonah Bell, but why are you asking me? You are the head of our household."

"I wanted to see how you felt, since you will be feeding another mouth each night, and that would take time away from just the three of us. John is older, but he is strong, and he could live quite a few more years."

"Well, I should hope so. You know I don't mind John being here. I agree that he should not have to be alone."

"Good, then it is settled. We shall build a cabin and move John here to live out his life. And another thing. Since we are talking, I was thinking about putting up a curtain across there," Jonah motioned with his hand, "to close off our bed from the rest of the cabin."

Savannah looked at him quickly, as she remembered her mother saying a curtain was put up because a man had his needs.

"Why would you want to do that?" Savannah could not imagine why *Jonah* would want to block off their bed, the way he kept his distance.

"That way if you decide to go to bed early and John was still here, you could excuse yourself, and we would not bother you."

She was puzzled. "Since when do I ever go to bed before you do?"

"I thought you might like your privacy," Jonah shrugged his shoulders.

"A curtain would be nice, though. It would be like having another room. So, I agree it's a good idea, but not because I'd want to go to bed early; unless of course, you wanted me to, so you men could talk."

"If we were going to talk about something I did not wish for you to hear, I would go outside," Jonah teased.

"Yes, I imagine you would."

"Would you mind reading the Bible while I work on the chain? It's been a couple of nights since you read, and I am sure Rose misses it."

"Well, Jonah, I never dreamed you would ask that of me. Has something happened to change your mind about God?" It made her happy he wanted her to read God's Word.

"Nothing particular, just thinking a lot about things, and life."

Savannah eagerly opened her Bible to Matthew and started to read.

Jonah loved to hear her read. He used to think it was because it reminded him of the nights Clara read from her Bible, but lately, that wasn't it at all. The truth was, there were so many unanswered questions, and if it were true there really was a God, and this was His word, then he had much to learn.

*****

"Savannah, get up," Jonah shook her lightly on her shoulder.

Savannah rubbed her eyes and looked sleepily at him. "Is something wrong with Rose?"

"Not at all. It's Christmas morning and Santa has come."

Savannah smiled. "I don't think I have ever seen you this excited."

"Come on, get up, it's Christmas."

Savannah climbed out of bed, wearing her long flannel gown her mother had made her their last Christmas together. "Are you going to wake up Rose, also?"

Jonah pointed to the other side of the cabin at Rose lying awake in her bed. "I woke her before you. Come on, girls, and come to the fire."

Savannah loved seeing Jonah this way. It was the first time she truly felt like part of the family. It brought back wonderful memories of when she was a little girl and her mother made Christmas special.

Rose crawled out of bed and ran eagerly to her father's arms. "Well, aren't you waking up in a great mood this morning," Jonah laughed. "Santa come last night, Rose, here have a seat." Jonah placed her in a chair and motioned for Savannah to sit also.

Jonah went to the tree and picked up two gifts he had sneaked in the night before, after they had gone to sleep, and handed one to each of them.

"What is this? I don't remember seeing this," her eyes were wide with excitement.

"Of course you don't remember it. I just told you, Santa brought it," Jonah winked at her.

"Oh, Santa. Open your gift from Santa, Rose. Let's see what he brought you."

Rose started to tear at the paper, "Santa," she said out loud, leaving Jonah and Savannah laughing at her eagerness to see what was inside the bright colored paper.

"Baby," Rose giggled, pulling out a porcelain doll and hugging it tightly.

"Oh, Jonah, it is beautiful," Savannah clapped. "It is even more beautiful than the one I had as a child. I will make it more clothes to wear, Rose, so you can play dress up. Would you like that?"

Rose got down from the chair and crawled back up in her bed, carrying the doll with her.

Jonah laughed. "I guess she isn't ready to get up just yet."

"Well, it is a bit early. It isn't even daylight," Savannah agreed.

"Go ahead, it's your turn, open your gift," Jonah couldn't wait for her to see what was inside.

She tore gently at the paper and gasped at the beautiful handmade box inside. "Oh Jonah, it is so beautiful. Did you make it?"

"I did. I wanted to make you something you could keep your mother's letters in. Go ahead and open it up," he urged.

She opened the box and screamed with excitement at the glass snowdome inside. It was the one she had looked at the mercantile. "It is beautiful, Jonah, I love it!"

"I thought you might like to have it for your own."

"Thank you, Jonah," she hugged him tightly. To her surprise, he returned the hug, without pulling away.

Now you sit down; it's my turn." Savannah pulled a box out from underneath the bed. "Open it."

Jonah smiled and opened the box. Inside was another new shirt with a new hat and scarf to match.

"When did you have time to do this without me seeing you make it?"

"Really, Jonah?" Savannah laughed. "You stay outside more than inside. I have plenty of time when you are not watching."

"I love it, Savannah; thank you so much for all you do for both Rose and I."

"You are welcome. I crocheted Rose a new blanket for her bed, but it looks like she will have to open it later," Savannah pointed at Rose, who had fallen back asleep, holding close to her new doll.

"Go look under the tree in the back," Jonah pointed. "I think I see one more box."

Savannah bent down to look more closely. "*Well,* there is another box under there! I wonder where it came from?"

"Why don't you open it and see what it is."

She picked up the box and came back to the table. "Jonah, you shouldn't have."

"Open it first, it might be something you wish I shouldn't have," he laughed.

Savannah knew this was by far the best Christmas she had ever had in all her life. Just to be here, in the warmth of the cabin with the most handsome man in the whole world. A man that was her husband, and this morning, Christmas morning, he was treating her as if she were his wife.

"Oh Jonah!" Savannah screamed. "You bought me new shoes! Do you know how long it's been since I had a pair of new shoes?"

"Much too long, I am guessing. Go ahead and try them on."

Savannah slid the shoes on her feet and stood. "They fit perfect, how did you know?"

"I measured your shoes while you were sleeping. They look good on you."

"They are wonderful. The best shoes I've ever had. I will save my old shoes to tend animals and work outside, and I will wear these for dressing up and going into town."

"So, you like your gifts?"

"Yes Jonah, they are wonderful. Thank you so much." Savannah hugged him again.

"Thank you for making Christmas special."

Savannah hoped that one day soon he would be able to give her the gift she longed for, and that was the gift of his heart.

*****

One of Savannah's favorite chores was gathering the eggs every day, especially since the snow had melted, and springtime had once again come to the valley.

"Do you think this is a good spot?" Jonah shouted out, pointing to a place on the left side of the house, in the opposite direction of the outhouse.

"I think that is a grand spot, indeed," Savannah answered, shutting the door to the pen and walking toward him with Rose on her heels.

"Then I shall get started today. When I am finished, we shall all go together and fetch him."

"And what if he doesn't want to come? Don't you think we should ask him first?"

"No," he disagreed. "I've already asked, remember, and he said no. If we all go together and already have the cabin built, he can't possibly say no."

"And what if he comes for a visit before you finish it?" she loved seeing Jonah brainstorm through this task to bring a lonely man to live with them.

"Then I shall say I am building a workshop."

"Do you think he will believe that when you have the barn and the shed already?"

Jonah laughed. "Only a woman would think such thoughts. Trust me, if he comes around before I am finished, he will believe whatever I tell him."

"Okay, if you trust that to be so."

"I do. So how many eggs did you get?"

Savannah investigated her apron full of eggs and counted. "We gathered sixteen."

"And you gathered that amount yesterday, too. It looks like it is about time to start trading eggs as well as skins. God is so good to us."

Had she heard Jonah say what she thought he said? "He is, Jonah. He surely is."

Maybe there was hope for him, after all, she giggled to herself. If she can't have him, at least God could.

*****

"Water, Momma, play in water." Rose had been begging to go outside and play in the creek since breakfast.

"Okay then, let me grab my journal and we shall go. I can write, and watch Jonah finish the cabin while you play."

Savannah leaned back against the tree trunk and opened her journal. The end of May was such a beautiful time of year.

The tiny cabin is coming to life. Jonah has worked so very hard to have his friend a place to stay close to us.

I do think John reminds Jonah of his own father that passed long ago.

Jonah has been through a lot in his life. More than most men and it is no wonder he is the way he is, not wanting to get too close.

I have already made the curtain to place on the one window that will face our own cabin and cannot wait to place it and make the tiny cabin look like a home.

Rose is a little older than two years old and growing so fast. I think the name Rattle-Box suits her a lot more than me. I do so wish my mother could see her grandbaby, she would love her every bit as much as I do.

It's nice to see the bond that Jonah and Rose have finally formed. She rushes to his arms every time he comes in from the day's work, as if she has not seen him in such a long time.

It's been over two years since we wed and even though Jonah seems to care deeply for me, I have still yet to hear the words, "I love you." Oh, how I long to hear Jonah say that to me.

At least he is now telling Rose. Every child needs to know they are loved.

I received another letter from mother last week. She is still sewing and finding things to do to help father earn an income.

If I could only be half as ambitious as mother, I would make Jonah so proud. I sometimes wonder if he wishes he chose someone else to be his wife. Maybe by now he would have loved her too.

Even though I am happy being his wife and Rose's mother, my heart cries out just to know what it would be like to have him truly love me. At least after all this time I have grown accustomed to the fact that may never be, and for the most part I am happy just being in his presence. Jonah is truly my best friend.

CHAPTER 12

Savannah stood back and inspected the cabin that was to be John's. Everything had come together nicely, from the curtain on the window to the bed Jonah had made. He even allowed her to use one of Clara's quilts, and it was the finishing touch to make it look like a home.

"He is going to love it, Jonah!" Savannah beamed. "When can we go get him? It's already June, and I am starting to worry. He should have already gone into town by now to pick up supplies, and I am certain he would never pass without stopping for a meal and a hello."

"I feel the same. I know he was here with us for several months, and with all the extra goods we sent back with him that would do him a while, but I was certain he would have been back before now. Let's go tomorrow. I think we are ready here," Jonah put his arm around Savannah and admired the tiny cabin.

It pleased her the way Jonah was slowly starting to show small signs of affection. "You have done a great job building John a house."

"And you, my dear wife, have taken that house and made it a home. We make a good team."

Savannah smiled. "Yes, we do."

*****

It was a beautiful day to be picking John up. Hot, but beautiful.

The thick forest around them was full of different sorts of trees, and the growth of leaves was once again full this time of year.

Rose screamed and pointed at a groundhog scurrying by. "Momma, look!"

"It's a groundhog, Rose," Savannah laughed. She loved her excitement upon seeing something new.

"I hope we are able to find his cabin. He told me he lived toward the south," Jonah said.

"I was just thinking that Rose and I have never been in this direction. How far away did he say he lived?"

"Far enough that we will need to stay there tonight and start back in the morning."

"It's good we brought the bed rolls." She was excited about their adventure. Just to be able to get out and go to an unknown territory was exciting.

"I think he will be most happy to see the meal you prepared and brought with us," Jonah chuckled.

"It's merely rabbit stew and cornbread."

"And fried apple pies," Jonah added.

"I do hope he wants to come, and you have not built a cabin to go to waste."

"It would never be a waste. One cannot get enough extra space. I was just thinking, we need to prepare ourselves for what we may find."

"What do you mean, Jonah?"

"It's been almost a year since we have seen him. I am second guessing if I should have brought you and Rose along."

Savannah put her hand to her lips and gasped. "Oh, Jonah, do you think something could be wrong?"

"I pray not, but I want to go in first to make sure."

Savannah had not thought of that, that perhaps John might have passed away, and no one would have known. "I pray not also.

I am sure he is fine. Like you said, he still had a lot of supplies by being with us all those months and we did send him home with plenty. I am glad you brought us along, for if it is something bad you do not need to face it by yourself. I want to be here for you." Savannah placed her hand on top of his, and for the first time, he turned his hand and took hold of hers.

"If I don't say it enough, and I know I don't, I am so grateful for all you do for Rose and me. I know I could have never made it out west with my daughter, if it not been for you. You make our house a home each and every day."

"Thank you for saying that. I appreciate your kind words." She squeezed his hand a bit tighter, loving the way her hand felt in his rough calloused hand.

"You are the most patient woman I ever met, and you have taught me to believe in God again."

Savannah felt the tears pooling in her eyes. "Oh Jonah, if that be the case, and I never do anything else for you, I feel I have done what God wanted me to accomplish."

"You never once gave up or cowed down. You kept right on reading God's Word night after night and praying out loud. Your faith astounds me."

"God has been good to me in my life. I have no reason not to have faith in Him."

"I also want to apologize again for whisking you up and bringing you so far away from your family without so much as asking what you thought about it."

"As a woman, I am aware that I don't always get to have a say in such matters, and even though it was a shock when mother first told me the news, I have never wished I was still back in Georgia, and not with you and Rose."

Jonah looked her way and smiled. "Do you *really* mean that?"

"Of course, I do."

"*But* you did not even know me, Savannah, nor my child."

"I knew you, Jonah, just not personally." Perhaps it was time to tell Jonah the truth.

"We never spoke, just passed each other from time to time." She slid a bit closer to him and hoped what she was about to say would help their relationship, instead of making it worse.

"Do you know the guilt you felt for taking me on as your wife just a few weeks after Clara had gone to be with Jesus?"

Jonah was not sure he wanted to remember that moment but was curious to see what Savannah needed to say. "Yes, I sometimes wish I could forget it."

"I live with guilt too, Jonah. As a Christian who loves our Lord, I live with guilt, too."

Jonah furrowed his brow, having no idea what this angelic woman would ever have done. "I cannot imagine anything you ever did that you would feel guilty about."

"It isn't anything I did, Jonah, it was thoughts I had, and doesn't God's Word tell us that our thoughts can also be sins of the flesh?"

"You had thoughts of hurting me, did you?" he chuckled. "I can't say as I blame you."

"Jonah, this is not funny. I am trying to express something to you."

Jonah could see the seriousness on her face and shook his head. "I am sorry, please forgive me for joking about something like that. Please go on."

"Thank you. I first saw you at the mercantile in Dahlonega, they called it Talonega then. I was fourteen at the time. You did not see me, but I followed you, hiding from your sight, to listen to you talk to the proprietor. You told him that you moved there to find gold with your wife. I watched you for a long time that day. I saw you go to the blacksmith and have your horse shod and to pick up lumber to build you and Clara a bed."

"I am not sure what to say. I remember that day well."

"That was not the only time I watched you. As the months went on, I would watch you plow in the field from afar, and I would hide behind the great oak at Mill's Pond and watch you pass."

"And you watched me because…?" Jonah was still confused.

"Because I thought you were the most handsome man I ever laid eyes on," Savannah sighed. She had finally said it, after all this time.

Jonah chuckled again. "Me?"

"Jonah, you were a married man, very much in love with your wife, and I was merely a child with a longing to be near you. Just a glimpse from afar, and I was happy a few more days until I saw you again."

"So, you felt guilty because you thought I was handsome, and I was married?"

"It wasn't just that. It was the thoughts that raced through my head each time I watched you. I would secretly wish I was Clara and I could be your wife, and that you would love me the way you loved her."

"Wow, I just do not know what to say. I had no idea."

"Don't you see, Jonah? I was having thoughts that no one should have about a married man, nor unmarried, for that matter."

"So, when your mother told you that you were going to be my wife?"

"I was in shock, for just that day I had hid and watched you drive past. I did not know you were coming from my home and had just spoken to father about me. But I was also thrilled that my dream was coming true, and I would be your wife."

"And after all this time, are you still thrilled? If you knew it would turn out this way, would you still be thrilled?"

"I would, because even though I fear I may never experience real love from you, the way every woman desires, I get to spend my life by your side. Jonah, you are the only man I would have ever wanted to grow old with."

"And if Clara had not passed?"

"Then I guess I would have sneaked glances of you until you moved far away, and I would have thought about you all the days of my life."

Jonah sat in silence for a moment, thinking of all she had said. If she truly felt this way, all the distance on his part must be unbearable at times. She had never had a love like he and Clara had, and he now realized that he *was* her first love, just as Clara was his.

"Savannah?" Jonah said softly, after some time had passed.

"Yes, Jonah?"

"Why did you tell me this now?"

She shrugged. "I felt it was time. I did not wish for you to live out your life thinking I did not desire to be with you."

He shook his head in thought.

"Jonah, are you terribly upset with me? Please know I never wanted or wished that Clara would pass; I merely desired to know how she felt. What it would be like to be your wife."

"I am not upset, Savannah. Thank you for sharing your thoughts with me. It means a lot to me. So how do you now feel about being my wife?'

I love being your wife, Jonah. I may not know how Clara felt, because she had a part of you I shall never have. She had your heart. But I do love being your wife and Rose's mother more than you can ever know."

*****

A couple of hours before dark a small cabin came into view. Jonah recognized John's wagon and knew he was in the right place.

The cabin was old and run down, and weeds were growing waist-deep all around. What once was a barn had fallen in on one side, and it appeared no one had lived there for quite some time.

"Savannah, I want you and Rose to stay put. Do not get down until I come back for you."

"Oh Jonah, I fear the worst. Do you think John moved somewhere else without telling us? It appears no one is here."

"Here or not, we are going to have to stay here for the night. I will come back for you." Jonah got down from the wagon and started for the door. His biggest fear was finding that John had passed months ago, and he wasn't prepared for what he might find inside.

"John!" Jonah called out, opening the door slowly. "Are you home? It's me, Jonah. I come to visit you."

The cabin was dark, and Jonah allowed his eyes to adjust so he could get a good look around. In the corner he could see a bed and what looked like someone covered with an old quilt.

"John, is that you?" Jonah asked, coming closer, fearing the worst.

Slowly he pulled back the blanket and heard John moan. He was burning up with fever.

"John, it's me, Jonah. I am here to help you, buddy."

"Jonah?" John said, confused. "Ye need to go and not risk getting sick."

"You are my friend, John. I will not leave you. Let me get Savannah."

Jonah took off for the wagon. "John is very sick with fever. I am not sure he will make it."

Savannah jumped off the wagon without waiting for him to help her." Fetch me some water and build a fire. Stay away from John and keep Rose away. You two can head back in the morning. You can sleep in the wagon tonight. Leave me here for the week, then come back and fetch me."

"Savannah, you can't stay here alone. Did you not hear what I just said? John is very sick. If we could get it, you could very well get it also."

"I will take my chances. I know what I am doing, Jonah, I have seen mother take care of people numerous times. You must go back and tend the livestock. Give me a week to see if I can nurse him back to health."

Without hesitating, Jonah rushed in to start a fire and brought in water from the creek nearby.

Savannah went right to work placing cold rags on John's head and face and forcing him to take sips of cold water.

"Savannah, please go," John whispered. "It is too late for me."

"You hush now, John, I will not listen to negative talk from you. You *are* going to make it. Do you hear me?"

After several hours, darkness had taken over. She set a bowl of rabbit stew out on the porch for Jonah and Rose to eat, and tried to keep her distance as she spoke to him. "Please go back with Rose at first light. I am sorry you will have to tend her until you come back for me, but I am not sure what this is and do not wish to take chances with her, since she is so young."

"But Savannah, what about you?"

"I will do all I can to help him. I am so glad we came today. I am not sure he would have made it till morning. I am trying to give his body some nourishment and bring down the fever that plagues him."

"I meant what about you? What will keep you from getting sick as well?"

Savannah moved closer to the door, so he could see she had a rag over her nose and mouth. "I will do all I can to not get sick as well. And I will pray to my Father to help me."

"I hate leaving you out here all alone."

"I am not alone, Jonah. John is with me, and most of all, God. He cannot go back this way; he must get better first. If we all leave him like this, he will surely die, for he is not strong enough to fight it off alone."

"I will do as you wish and trust in God to make things right. I will be back for you this time next week. Do you have enough food here?"

"Yes, he still has some of the food I sent home with him, and there is some flour and meal."

"I do not see his horse or cow. I have looked everywhere. What will you do for milk? "We will drink water. I can go fetch more at the creek. Please do not worry. I am going to be okay; just pray for John to get stronger."

Savannah closed the door and locked it, knowing at first light Jonah and Rose would be gone.

Dear Father,
If I have ever needed you before, it is now. Please Father, help me nurse John back to health. I am begging of you not to take him this way.

Father, you said that by Your stripes we are healed. You have made the blind see and the lame walk, and I am trusting that you will bring down this fever and heal his weak body back to health.
Amen

Savannah lit the oil lamps and tried to tidy up the cabin as best she could before she ate a small portion of rabbit stew herself, realizing it was the first thing she'd eaten since daylight.

Over and over she wet the rags in cold water and placed them on John's head and face. Savannah even removed his wet shirt covered in sweat and wiped him down with the cool water in hopes to bring down the fever.

Finding an old tattered Bible on the hearth above the fireplace, Savannah pushed over a rocking chair by John's bed and began to read the scriptures of the miracles Jesus had performed, reminding Him of His promises.

*****

Savannah only nodded off a time or two during the night, trying not to get into a deep sleep for fear of leaving John unattended for too long.

As much as she worked throughout the night, she knew it could be days before he was out of the woods completely, and on his way to being stronger and feeling well enough to take the day's journey back to his new cabin that was waiting for him.

Savanah decided not to mention it to John, but to wait until Jonah returned with Rose, so they could both tell him together.

Looking around the old dusty cabin, Savannah envisioned a time when Martha was still alive and had made it a home.

How sad it must be for John to lose his heart and inspiration. It was easy to see that loneliness had set in months ago, and he had given up. What was the reason to fix things, when no one was there but himself?

Savannah looked out the window at daybreak and watched their wagon as it disappeared through the forest of trees.

Go with them, Father, and keep them safe. Send Your angels to guard them and protect them on their journey home, and please, Father, cast your healing over this house and remove this sickness as far as the east is from the west.
In Jesus' Name,
Amen.

CHAPTER 13

It was strange going into the cabin without Savannah, and Jonah knew immediately that his house would never be a home without her presence.

"Momma," Rose started crying the moment they walked in the door.

"It's going to be okay, Rose. We are going back to get Momma in a few days."

"Momma!" she wailed. Never had she cried this way before. In the past, at the slightest whimper, Savannah would rush to her and pick her up and take her to the rocking chair to console.

Jonah picked her up and carried her to the rocker, which did not have the same effect on her as when Savannah rocked her. As hard as Rose could, she kicked and screamed for her momma.

"Well, Savannah, we did not think this through," Jonah said aloud. "Hush now, sweet girl, Momma will be home soon; it's going to be all right."

After ten minutes of outburst, Rose cried herself to sleep, and Jonah gently placed her in her bed.

It wasn't easy pulling the wagon away from John's house, knowing with every mile they traveled they were that much farther away from Savannah.

He went back outside to unhitch the team and feed the other livestock while Rose slept. He knew it was not going to be an easy week without Savannah; not only because she did so much for them both, but more than ever he realized just how much he was going to miss her.

*****

Savannah gathered water from the creek that ran beside John's home.

Looking around his farm, she could tell that it was once beautiful and alive. She wondered when it was that he had given up. He'd been so strong when he came to help them build the barn and the fence. It was hard to believe he would let his place run down so.

Two days had passed since Jonah left her and it felt like weeks. Oh, how she missed him and Rose, and she wondered how they were faring.

John moaned out loud as she entered the cabin. "Are you okay, John?" He had not spoken to her in two days, but instead seemed to be in a deep sleep.

"Thirsty," he whispered.

She smiled; it was the first improvement she had noticed since the night she arrived. "Yes sir, let me get you some water."

Savannah got the ladle and dished him out some of the cold water from the bucket and placed it near his mouth. John drank quickly and asked for more.

"Let's not drink too much at once. Just a little more. I am heating you up some broth; that should give you nourishment. I am glad you are finally awake to drink and eat. I was very worried about you."

"Where is Jonah?" John asked softly, barely a whisper.

"He took Rose and went back to our cabin. They will be back in a few days to get me." "They left ye here?" John seemed confused.

"Yes, I told them to. You needed a nurse. I am not a nurse, but I was all you had given the circumstances. If you continue to drink and eat the broth for the next couple of days, I will cook you a nice meal. Let's get your strength back first, though."

"Ye should not have stayed."

"Hush up now, you would have done the same for me; in fact, you did. I do remember you staying with us for months helping us around the farm."

John tried to smile but only coughed and winced in pain. "Sorry."

"Sorry for what? Getting sick? That's not your fault. How long have you been sick?"

"Don't remember. I thought I was going to die."

"And you very well might have if Jonah had not wanted to come visit you. It has been so long since we seen you last, and we were worried."

"Horse died," John breathed in heavy. "I just didn't think I could make that walk on foot."

"Where is your cow? The one you brought to the house with you?"

"She died too. Barn fell in after the first blizzard," he coughed.

"Oh, John, I am so sorry."

"It's life."

"So how are you feeling now?"

"Like a hammer hit my head," he smiled weakly.

"I can imagine. I am sorry I do not have anything for the pain. I pray that in the next couple of days you start feeling much better. I think the broth will do you good."

"I feel so tired."

"Your body needs to heal. Go back to sleep, and I will wake you later to drink a bit of broth."

"Could you read to me some more?"

Savannah reached for the Bible. "I wasn't aware that you heard me."

John nodded his head. "God's Word is comforting."

"I agree, and I will be happy to read. Just close your eyes and rest."

Even though John wasn't totally out of the woods yet, for the first time she felt hope.

*****

Rose calmed down and stopped asking for momma by the third day. It took that long for Jonah to convince her that they were going back for momma in a few days.

By the fifth day, Jonah learned several things about himself.

He was not cut out to be a momma and did not know the first thing about cooking. He was grateful Savannah had made up plenty of bread before she left, and he could always fry meat.

Of course, the thing he hated most about her being gone was not something he would have ever thought about before; he was once again sleeping alone.

For over two years now, he'd slept beside her, and even though there had been no intimacy, she was there. Just to hear her breathe was comforting.

He stretched his arm across the bed and felt the coolness of the material without her warm body upon it.

Rose had been sleeping for hours, and tonight, like every night since Savannah had not been there, he was finding it hard to sleep.

He was not lying awake missing Clara, as he had so many nights after she passed, but instead, he was missing Savannah. Everything about her was beautiful, and she deserved so much more than he gave her.

He thought about what she had told him on the ride to John's and how she must feel, night after night, longing for him to reach out to her and pull her close.

He knew he'd been selfish, and it pained him. It pained him because not pulling her close was pushing her away in a sense, and he wondered how she must feel after all this time.

Did she desire him more, or did his selfishness make her see him differently?

From the very beginning, he'd never seen her as a child, but as a beautiful young woman who always looked older than her age.

It was never that she wasn't good enough or beautiful enough, but that his heart belonged to another woman, a woman he was not able to let go.

But now? Now that so much time had passed, he found himself going days without thinking about Clara at all, and there were times he had to think hard to even remember what she looked like. At those times, he would look into Rose's eyes, and there he would find her, his Clara.

But Clara did not belong to him any longer; she belonged to God now, just as she always had.

Till death do us part. He had heard those words over and over since John's talk with him that night, which now seemed like so long ago.

And John was right; the pledge he had made to Clara was broken by those words and gave him freedom to love another.

Until now, Jonah had never wanted to love another. But tonight, here in the dark of their cabin and the loneliness he felt with Savannah gone, he realized more than ever that he did love another. He was not sure quite when it had happened, but it did, nevertheless.

*****

"That was a mighty tasty meal, Savannah. I just cannot thank ye enough for all that ye did for me." John was now sitting up in bed and eating solid foods.

"You are welcome; it is my pleasure."

"How many days has it been?"

"Six. Jonah and Rose will be here tomorrow, if I have calculated right."

"I will be glad to see them, as I am sure ye will be also."

"Yes, I am happy the week is almost over; not that I mind being here with you, but you have not been the best company, I am afraid," she giggled.

"Do ye realize this is the second time ye both saved my life?"

"It was God that saved you John, not us."

"But God sent ye both to help me."

She nodded. "Isn't it nice the way God works, always loving us and working on our behalf?"

"Yes, God is good."

"Can I ask you something, John?"

"Yes."

"When was it you give up?"

John looked around the cabin for a moment and thought about her question. "When the first blizzard hit, it caused my barn to fall. I didn't realize it was so weak, but I guess the years had taken a toll.

"If I had realized soon enough, I would have asked Jonah to help me fix it, but of course the blizzard was bad, and I could have never made it that far, and a blizzard has a way of getting a man lost very quick, so I had to stay put."

"I'm so sorry, John."

"It seemed that there was one snow after another, and by the time I was finally able to make my way to the barn, it was too late. Made me feel terrible not being able to save them. Snow was so deep I couldn't get out."

"It was a terrible winter, for sure."

"In the springtime, I buried them and decided I'd eat the rest of the food I had and would just die. Problem was I had more than I thought, staying with ye those months and not using my own supplies, and then all that ye sent back with me."

She nodded. "After hearing this story, I am glad we did. God was not ready for you to die."

"When I found myself sick, I went to bed and prayed God would take me on to be with Martha. If I recollect right, I am almost seventy years old. I have no right to even still be here."

"The good Lord won't take you until He is ready. He still has a plan for your life."

John shook his head sadly. "I can't imagine what that is. When ye are my age with an old cabin, a collapsed barn, and not even a horse to speak of, what else is there? I live too far away from the village to walk for supplies, and certainly cannot carry them on my back to get them home."

"We can help you, John. We would love to help you."

"Ye see how far it is from my house to yours, and it isn't right for the two of ye to worry about the likes of me. Ye are both young and have such an amazing life ahead of you. I am not going to be the one to stand in the way of that."

Savannah took a deep breath and let it out slow. Oh, how she wished that were true, but for the life of her it could never be an amazing life if Jonah could not let go of Clara's memory long enough to give her his heart.

"We love you, John, you know that."

He smiled. "And I love ye both also. Ye are the children I was never blessed to call my own."

*****

Jonah's heart skipped a beat when he and Rose rounded the corner and John's cabin came into sight. "Giddy up," he yelled, willing the horses to go faster the last couple of miles.

"Whoa," he stopped close to the front door and called out for her, "Savannah!"

Savannah came out on the porch smiling that beautiful smile that melted his heart. Jonah jumped off the wagon and rushed to her arms, lifting her up and spinning her around.

She laughed, "Goodness Jonah, you act like you missed me."

"That is putting it mildly. I am not cut out to be a momma and a housekeeper and a cook."

"Oh, I see now why you missed me."

"How is John?" he asked, placing her small body back on the porch floor.

"He is better, still in bed, but sitting up and eating. I told him he can get out of bed tomorrow."

"That's the best of news. I have prayed so hard."

"I am so glad you prayed, Jonah. I could feel your prayers."

"Momma!" Rose screamed from the wagon.

"Oh goodness, sweet girl, how are you?" Savannah rushed to her and lifted her in her arms. "I have missed you terribly. Did you miss me?"

Jonah laughed out loud. "That is a story for another day," he said, remembering how she had cried for two days straight.

"Go on in, John is eager to see you. And Jonah?"

"Yes?"

"I have not told him about the cabin yet. I wanted us to do that together."

Jonah could see from the moment he entered the cabin that Savannah had been there. Everything was clean and smelled of fresh bread.

"Well, hello," John said, sitting up in the bed. "I would have met ye at the door but ye wife says I have to wait until tomorrow to get up."

"And she knows best," Jonah laughed. "It is so good to see you doing better. You had me worried a week ago."

"I told ye wife this makes twice ye two have saved my life."

"You would have done the same for us. I have something to talk to you about," Jonah pulled a chair close to the bed and motioned for Savannah to sit in the rocker with Rose. John coughed and shook his head. "I imagine ye are going to fuss at me for letting my place get so run down."

"Not at all. In fact, I have a solution to all our problems."

John rubbed his whiskered face. "Well let's hear it, then," he chuckled, glad to see Jonah once again.

"Do you think you are up for the ride back to the cabin?"

"Ye mean your cabin?" John was confused.

"Yes."

"I lost my horse, Jonah. I would have no way back unless ye brought me."

"Well, I was thinking that we would not bring you back."

"Jonah, we have spoken on this before. There is not enough room in ye cabin for me, and I am not sure my old body could hold out long in the shed, but I do thank ye for caring. As soon as I am up again, I will try to start doing a little bit around here. Savannah has the place looking nice, doesn't she?"

Jonah looked at Savanah and smiled, and then back to John. "You are right about what you said. The cabin just isn't big enough for four of us, and the shed would be way too cold in the winter. Besides, who puts their long-term guests in a shed to live?"

Savannah giggled, excited for what Jonah was about to say.

"John, Savannah and I have built you a cabin on our land, close to our own cabin."

"What? Ye built me a cabin?"

"Yes. It isn't as big as ours, but it is big enough and has a fireplace to heat by. You can come to our house to eat meals with us, and on days you don't feel like venturing out, we will bring your meals to you."

John looked from Savannah to Jonah. "I do not understand."

"What is there to understand? Tomorrow we will set out and go back to the cabin and to your new home to live by us for as long as you shall live."

A tear fell from John's withered face, and he wiped it quickly away. "But why? Why would you do this? I am nothing to you."

Savannah reached and took his rough hand. "That is not so, and you know it. Was it not you that said we are like the children God never blessed you with?"

"She is right," Jonah spoke up. "We care about you. I had you on my mind all winter, and now I know why. As soon as spring hit, we started building. We were coming last week to get you but found you sick."

John looked up to the roof and spoke out loud. "Martha," he cried, "I'm not coming to see you as soon as I thought; it looks like my days here on this earth are not over yet."

"Papa John," Rose called out, making Savanah and Jonah laugh.

"See," Jonah said, "Even Rose claims you."

CHAPTER 14

John stood inside the cabin door of his new home. Never in his life had anyone given him such a gift as this.

Until now, he'd only been loved by Martha, and up until a week ago felt he had nothing to live for.

He opened his mouth to speak and closed it again. There just were no words to explain his gratitude.

Jonah placed his hands on John's shoulders and pulled him into an embrace. He could feel John's body shake as he cried.

"There is no need for words. Welcome home, buddy, welcome home."

"I will earn my keep, Jonah; ye will see there is still some good left in me."

"I did not bring you here to earn your keep. You already earned a lifetime when you helped me build the barn and fence. Just be happy, that's all I ask."

He smiled, wiping his tear-stained face. "I am certain I have never been this happy since Martha's death. Thank ye, Jonah, thank ye."

"You are welcome. Savannah and I can't have our parents with us as hers live too far away and mine have passed. Rose needs a Papa John, which is what I meant when I said I found a way to solve all our problems."

John chuckled, "I love that little girl."

"And she loves you. Enjoy your new home and please, never think you are bothering us. We expect you to come to the house often, especially at meal time."

*****

Jonah walked back to the house, whistling. It seemed life was finally working itself out. He was glad Savannah had taken Rose in the cabin and let him show John his new home. She had known it would be an emotional moment for him. She was wise beyond her years, and Jonah could see it more each day.

Savannah was at the woodstove, stirring a pot of beans.

The house smelled good again, the way it only could if she was there.

Rose drew pictures at the table and was content to have her momma close, just as she had been close since she was a tiny infant.

"Smells good," Jonah said, placing his hat on the rack.

"Just beans and cornbread, and I thought I would fry some potatoes. John loves those."

"John loves anything you cook," he laughed.

"Did he like the cabin?"

"Yes, he loved it. He's a little overwhelmed, but he will get used to it in time."

"I can understand that. You are a very good man, Jonah Bell, a very good man."

"And you are a very good woman. You saved his life Savannah, you know that."

"No, Jonah, it was God that spared his life, and *you* that listened to His voice that sent us there to fetch him."

"After dinner tonight, when John leaves and Rose is sleeping, I'd like to talk to you about something I've been thinking about while you were gone."

Savannah looked up from peeling potatoes with curiosity. "Okay, I would like that."

"And what I said yesterday, about the reason I missed you. I want you to know I did not just miss you because of the things you do around here."

She smiled. "Thank you, I appreciate you saying that. We will talk later tonight."

*****

John leaned back in his chair and rubbed his stomach as he always did after one of Savannah's meals. "I still cannot believe that I am going to be eating like this for the rest of my life. Maybe I died last week and went to heaven," he laughed.

"If you think my cooking is good, I wish you could have eaten from my mother's table; she was such a wonderful cook."

"If it got any better, I would not be able to stand myself," John teased.

"Papa John," Rose said, taking his hand. "Come play."

John got up from the table and followed Rose to her blocks. "Do ye want to build something?"

"Yes," she clapped. "Papa John build a house."

Jonah and Savannah smiled, watching the two of them play together. This was the way it should be. Rose had a Papa John, and John would no longer be lonely.

"I think I will wash the dishes before the Bible reading. That way we can have our talk later," Savannah said, getting up to clear the table.

"Sounds good. I will go tend the animals and be back shortly. Looks like Papa John has Rose occupied for now."

*****

Savannah was working on a crocheted blanket when Rose finally went to sleep that evening. John excused himself shortly after the Bible reading, saying he was tired. Savannah could hardly believe that he'd made it as long as he had, considering how sick he was just a few days before.

Jonah covered Rose up in Clara's quilt and sat down beside Savannah. "You are very talented, Savannah."

"Crocheting isn't that hard, Jonah."

"It's not just crocheting; it's everything. You are just magic."

"Magic," she laughed. "What do you mean?"

"Everything you touch turns to gold. Look at how Rose has turned out. She adores you, her momma. Do you know she cried for you two days after we left you?"

"Oh, Jonah, that is terrible."

"And look at how you made this house a home. It was a miserable place here without you."

"With Rose crying for two days, I can imagine it was," she winked.

"It wasn't just that, Savannah. I missed you. I missed you like I never thought I would."

"It isn't easy doing all my chores and yours too, Jonah. I am sorry I had to send you back like that, but we could not take any chances that Rose might get sick; she is just too young to fight it off."

"I don't mean that. Sure, it wasn't easy doing all you do in a day, which I never realized until I had to do it. What I meant was I *missed* you."

"But you knew I was coming back. You had not lost me, like you lost Clara."

"I did not think of Clara at all, Savannah. I could not stop thinking about *you*."

Savannah looked toward him and never missed a stitch. "I wonder why?" She needed to hear him say it.

Jonah took both hands and ran them through his thick black hair. "There are days when I cannot remember what she looked like, Savannah."

"I am so sorry, Jonah. You say Rose looks just like her. You can remember her through your daughter."

"And that is what I do each time I forget. I look at her, and that helps me remember."

"I'm sorry that Clara is not here with you now. I am sorry that you have had to go through so much pain. I am sorry that you had to marry me to take care of your daughter."

"Don't be sorry, Savannah," Jonah swallowed, knowing what he was about to say could change their relationship forever. "I am not sorry at all that I married you."

"You aren't?"

He slid the chair closer to her and took her hand in his. "I'm sorry that I have pushed you away so many times. I am sorry that I have taken you for granted. I am sorry if I have treated you as anything less than my wife. Please forgive me."

"It's okay, Jonah, I know why you married me. If it had not been for Rose, you still would not be married. I know you, Jonah, and I know how faithful you are to your love, to Clara. You do not have to explain to me."

"Yes, I do have to explain. I have been doing a lot of soul-searching the past week. I have searched my heart and realize that Clara no longer owns it."

"What do you mean?" She could feel herself starting to tremble.

"I am not sure exactly when it happened, Savannah, but slowly you started owning my heart, and I did not realize how deeply it went until I left you at John's, with him sick, and I feared that you might also get sick and that I could possibly lose you."

"What are you saying, Jonah?"

"I have fallen in love with you, Savannah. So deeply in love with you, it hurts."

She gasped. "Oh Jonah, please don't say it if you don't mean it."

He smiled. "I mean it, Savannah. I love you. I love you every bit as much as I loved Clara."

"But I never wanted to take her place. I just wanted you to love me, too."

"And I do. Savannah, I love you. Will you please do me the honor of being my wife?"

Savannah giggled through tears. "I am already your wife."

"But I never asked you, not the way a lady should be asked."

"Yes, Jonah, I will be your wife."

Jonah stood and pulled Savannah to her feet. "Do you think you might ever love me half as much as I love you? He smiled that sexy smile that made her melt inside.

"I already love you more," she whispered.

Jonah pulled her close and pressed his lips to hers. The very taste of her was intoxicating, and he wanted her to melt in his arms.

Savannah moaned from the pleasure of his kiss, but unlike last time, he did not pull away.

"I love you too, Jonah. I think I have always loved you."

"Make love to me, Savannah. I want to be your husband and for you to be my wife."

Jonah picked her up and carried her to their bed. "I will be gentle, I promise."

"I have never been with a man, Jonah. I hope I do not disappoint you."

"How could you ever disappoint me, Savannah? You are my wife, and I love you so."

He kissed her again and she welcomed it. This was the way marriage was supposed to be. She prayed this day was real, and she would not wake to the sun, realizing it was only a dream.

*****

Savannah awoke before daylight, lying in Jonah's arms. "Did I wake you?" he asked.

"Are you awake already?"

"I've been awake most of the night, watching you sleep. You are so beautiful and sleep so peaceful."

"So, it wasn't a dream. You really do love me?"

He pulled her closer. "I really *do* love you. I am so glad we put the curtain up between our bed and the rest of the cabin. Rose is getting older and I am not sure how we would explain ourselves," he chuckled. "Because I do not intend to sleep on the edge of the bed any longer."

"Yes, that would not be easy to explain, and I am so glad you feel that way. I love sleeping in your arms."

"Did I hurt you—last night, I mean?" The last thing he wanted to do was hurt her.

"No. Making love with you was more wonderful than I ever imagined."

"I am sorry I have waited so long. I have been up all night thinking about things."

"What kind of things?" she asked.

"I thought that afterwards, I would feel guilty, like I'd cheated on Clara, but I don't, Savannah, I don't."

"Does this concern you?"

"No, it's just that all this time when I thought about you and this moment, I thought that I would feel guilty and hate myself afterwards, but I don't."

"That's good, then. I am glad."

"But the truth is, I am so afraid."

"What are you afraid of, Jonah?"

"I am afraid you will get with child." He knew he feared that the most.

"It's possible, yes. Do you not want other children?"

"I don't think I could bear it if I lost you the way I lost Clara. It would kill me this time."

"Jonah, hundreds of women have gone through childbirth and made it just fine."

"And hundreds didn't make it."

She shifted so she could look him in the eye. "Jonah, please don't allow your fear to stop you from touching me. It is so nice to be loved by you the way a woman desires to be loved."

"I don't think I could stop now if I wanted to," he said, rubbing her face gently with the tip of his finger.

"Good, because now that we have made love, I don't think I could take it if you pulled away again."

"I won't, Savannah. I couldn't if I wanted to."

*****

Fall made its way to the valley once again, and the leaves changed to the most beautiful shades of reds and yellows and browns.

Savannah loved the fall but hated the winter that followed it.

As she gathered eggs, she noticed the winds had been picking up a lot since morning. "Looks like a storm is coming," she told Rose, who was petting a baby chick. "Come, let's get back inside the house."

Jonah and John had been gone since early morning, making a trip into town for supplies. She had decided to stay home with Rose, if Jonah would take a letter to the post office and check to see if she had one waiting for her.

Just as she closed the door, the rain started to pour, and lightning pierced the sky. Maybe it was coming from the village, and that was the reason they had yet to make it home. She thought they should have been home at least an hour ago.

Dear Jesus, protect them from this terrible storm and keep them safe.

"Raining, Momma," Rose stood in a chair and looked out the window.

"Yes, it's raining, Pumpkin. Come down and go play." Savannah lifted her off the chair and sent her in the direction of her toys.

Savannah grabbed her Bible and started to read out loud. It was the only thing that seemed to comfort her when she was nervous.

The Lord is my Shepherd; I shall not want.

He maketh me to lie down in green pastures: he leadeth me beside the still waters.

He restoreth my soul: he leadeth me in the paths of righteousness for his name's sake. Yea, though I walk through the valley of the shadow of death, I will fear no evil: for thou art with me; thy rod and thy staff they comfort me.

Thou preparest a table before me in the presence of mine enemies: thou anointest my head with oil; my cup runneth over.

Surely goodness and mercy shall follow me all the days of my life: and I will dwell in the house of the Lord forever.

Savannah put her Bible down and started to pace the floor.

The storm made it almost dark outside, and it took her back to the time they were caught in the wagon in the storm.

Maybe Jonah and John would sleep in the wagon tonight and try to come the rest of the way in the morning. Surely, they could not ride in this.

The thunder boomed again, causing Rose to scream and run to her arms. "It's all right, Rose. It is just a storm."

Even though Savannah tried to comfort her, she understood how she was feeling. What if something happened to both Jonah and John?

How would she ever make it out here alone? She had no idea how to make it back to Dahlonega where her family lived, and would her father welcome her back with Rose? Why, oh why, was she thinking such thoughts, she scolded herself, pacing again across the floor, watching the trees sway back and forth. It was almost dark now.

"Come on Rose, let us go lay down. You can sleep with me tonight."

It wasn't long before Rose was fast asleep as the storm still raged.

She knew there would be no sleep for her tonight. Even if the storm stopped. Until Jonah and John were safe at home, she might never sleep again.

CHAPTER 15

Savannah watched daybreak come to the valley. The storm had stopped raging hours ago, but there was still no sign of Jonah and John.

Never had he made a trip into town and not made it back the same day. But then never had there been such a storm as the one last night.

Rose cried out from her bed before snuggling under the quilt and going back to sleep. She had sat in the rocker all night after Rose had gone to sleep and kept the fire going, reading from her mother's old Bible.

Dear Father,
Thank You for your blessings, for they are more than I could have ever imagined. Thank You for sending Jonah into my life, for he is the most wonderful husband, father and friend.
Thank You for sparing John's life each time he has come close to death, for you knew that Jonah needed an earthly father, and John needed a family.
Thank You for this precious gift of life, now asleep on my bed. May she grow up to be healthy and happy, with a family of her own.
Thank You for being with Jonah and John last night, for You, Father, are in the storm and I trust that you protected them from harm.

*Be with my family back home, Father, and keep them safe
and well.*
In Jesus' name,
Amen.

Savannah looked out the window to the land beyond, knowing
the direction Jonah would be coming from—still nothing.

*Maybe I will make some flapjack bread, it will be good with the
sorghum Jonah is bringing home.*

She knew keeping her mind and body busy would be the
only way she would keep from going crazy.

*****

The sun was high in the sky before Jonah's wagon came into
view. Savannah rushed outside at seeing them both return.

"Jonah, Jonah!" Savannah called out, as their wagon
approached the cabin. "Oh, Jonah, I was so worried about you
both."

He jumped off the wagon and rushed to her arms. "I'm so
sorry to make you worry, but I could not get back last night."

She felt like laughing and crying at the same time, her heart
pounding with joy and love. "I imagined all sorts of terrible
things. I have not slept all night."

"Did ye miss *me* much?" John asked, laughing. He loved
seeing Jonah and Savannah closing the distance he once saw.

She turned loose from Jonah and hugged him tightly. "Oh
yes, I missed you terribly much, Papa John," she laughed.

"Papa, Papa John," Rose screamed, jumping up and down.

"I guess this one had no trouble sleeping," Jonah joked.

"Not at all, she can sleep through anything. Did you bring
home the sorghum?"

"Two quarts, I did."

"Wonderful, come inside and eat. I've made flapjacks. It won't take long to whip up some eggs."

*****

It wasn't until later that evening that Savannah asked Jonah about the night before. Her favorite time for talking was after they'd gone to bed, and there was quietness around them. Just the two of them, lying in each other's arms, talking about their day.

"So, are you going to tell me what happened yesterday?"

"I was just waiting on you to ask," he chuckled.

She slapped at him playfully. "You knew I would wait until now. I wanted you to be able to speak freely, in case there was something you wanted to say away from John and Rose."

"I ran into your friend in town yesterday."

"My friend?" Savannah could not imagine who he meant.

Jonah laughed. "The lady that wears the tight dresses, from the saloon. She said to tell you hello."

Savannah frowned. "The nerve of her!" Savannah said angrily, making Jonah laugh.

"Did she really say that?"

"She did. Come right up to me when John was getting his hair cut and spoke."

"It looks like she and I are going to have to a have a talk. She knows you are *my* husband!" she snorted.

Jonah laughed and pulled her close. "Man, oh man, my wife has fire in her!"

"This is *not* funny, Jonah!" she giggled.

"I disagree. I think it is quite funny to see a jealous wife."

"I am *not* jealous."

"Oh, yes you are, and you know it."

She smiled and shook her head. "Well, maybe just a little. That woman gets on my nerves. She talks to me and looks at me as if I am not good enough for you and treats me like you could do much better. And by the way, she just happens to think you are so handsome, and she always makes it a point to tell me so."

"Is that so?" he grinned.

"Yes, every single time I am in the village. She is everywhere!"

Jonah chuckled. Oh, how he loved *this* woman. "Well, don't worry your pretty head, Savannah, you are much more beautiful than her any day of the week."

"Oh, you are just saying that because I am your wife."

He kissed her slowly and smiled. "No, I mean it. You are the most beautiful angel around these parts for hundreds of miles. I did good when I picked you for a wife."

She melted into his arms. "You say the sweetest things. I love you so, Jonah Bell."

"And I love you. And I'm sorry I could not get back, and that you worried about us."

"Wherever did you stay? Surely you did not stay with *her*?"

"Savannah, surely by now you know me better than that."

"I figured as much, but still had to ask," she joked.

"As we were headed out of town, I could see the storm closing in fast. I knew there would be no way we would make it back, so I stopped at the first place we came to and asked if we could perhaps wait it out in their barn."

"Oh, that was a clever idea. And what did they say?"

"Charles and Caroline Beasley are the nicest couple. He allowed us to drive our wagon right into the middle of their barn and sleep there in the hayloft."

"Did they feed you as well?"

"Yes, they brought us out fresh bread and butter and a bowl of stew."

"I am so happy they were there. I imagined all sorts of things but never imagined that."

He clucked his tongue, "Savannah, with as much faith as I know you have, I am surprised that you thought the worst."

"I usually don't, but however, when it comes to the man I love, my mind sometimes plays tricks on me."

"I can see that, and again I am sorry I caused you worry, but by the time the storm was over, it was much too dark to head back."

"Yes, I see that, but under the circumstances if the table were turned you would have worried about me."

"Yes, there is no doubt about that. I did not stop worrying even once when you were gone to John's."

"Well, then you know how I felt. At least you knew where I was."

"Didn't stop me from missing you any."

Savannah kissed him again. "This has become my favorite part of the day."

"It has, has it?" he grinned.

"Yes, it has. I love you, Jonah Bell." Savannah snuggled closer to him, so glad to have him home.

*****

Dear Mother,

I hope as always this letter finds you all well and happy.

I am happy to report that since I last wrote you, Jonah and I are finally living as husband and wife, and I could not be happier.

Jonah's only fear is that I will become with child and of course since Clara passed, he is afraid the same may happen to me.

I am not sure how to calm his fears, so please be praying for us and that he learns to have faith in God and realize some things are out of our control.

We built a small cabin on our land so that our neighbor could live close to us. He is a much older man; even older than you and father, and Jonah loves him as he would if he were his own father. I think it does Jonah good to have him close. Rose calls him Papa John.

Rose is growing so much now, Mother. She will be three years old soon and so very smart. I think I will start teaching her the alphabet soon, the way you did us.

Finally, she is using the chamber pot. No more nappies. What a blessing that is, especially in the winter time.

I am sorry I have not written to you in a while, it wasn't that I was not thinking about you. It is just that Jonah doesn't go for supplies as much as he used to since I put away so much food. It is nice though to always find a letter from you when he does get to go to the post office, and I will always try to mail you one back.

We were able to plant a lot of blueberry bushes and our apple trees are doing good, so I am hoping to make more jellies come spring and summer. I asked Jonah to look for some grape vines at the market in the spring, when he makes the next trip to the village.

So, I guess by the time you get this, we would have already gone through winter. The miles between us gets to me at times, and I wonder if I shall ever see you again?

I love you Mother; Please tell father and Mary I love them also. I have included a letter to Joseph.

Your daughter,
Savannah

*****

Winter brought a snowstorm that forced John to stay in the big cabin with the family, since Jonah insisted.

They carried his bed in just before it hit and got him settled.

"I hate I am intruding on ye two," John said, the first night he slept inside their cabin.

"Don't be silly, John, just look at the snow outside, and it doesn't look like it will be letting up anytime soon," Savannah handed him another cup of coffee.

"She's right," Jonah said, "It's going to be hard just getting out and in to tend the livestock, much less carry in wood to both places. Besides, it's much easier for us to all be together during this time."

"Ye two are much too good to me. I don't know what I ever did to deserve so much hospitality. Ye even built me a house," he grinned.

"And you come running when I needed you most, remember?" Jonah reminded.

"I have a confession to make," John spoke up.

"What is that, my friend?" Jonah asked, taking a sip of his coffee.

"It was for a selfish reason on my part, the reason I helped ye, that is. I was just so lonely and can't cook worth a flip, so I knew I would have company and get to eat good, too."

Savannah laughed. "That does not sound selfish to me at all; that sounds like a very smart man."

"She's right," Jonah agreed.

"Well, I must have done something right, 'cause just look at me now," John laughed. "I am one blessed man all right."

It was nights like this one that Savannah loved, with all the family sitting around the warm fire, telling stories of long ago.

How often her mind traveled back to when she was little, and winter would hit Talonega. A time before her brother and sister were born, when it was just her mother, father and herself.

"That's good, Savannah," Alice Bowen spoke up, referring to her name she was learning to write.

She was only six at the time and loved it when her mother was proud of her.

"My name has lots of letters," Savannah stated. "Eight letters."

"That's right, Savannah has eight letters. You are such a smart girl. I am so proud of you. Promise me that when you are older, you will teach your own children how to read and write. So many people today do not know how."

"Why, Mother?"

"Because they were never taught. Perhaps their mother did not know how, either. In any case, you will, and it isn't something you can keep to yourself; it must be shared."

"I promise, Mother."

"One day, Savannah, you could be living far away from me with your own family, and writing letters to each other could be our only way to communicate."

"I will never leave you, Mother. I love you too much."

Alice laughed and patted her on top of the head. "One can never know what tomorrow holds for them. One day, Savannah, you will be a beautiful grown woman, and you will meet a handsome man, and you will leave here and go make a life elsewhere."

"But Mother, I cannot cook."

Alice laughed. "Of course, you cannot now, but you will learn, and the more you cook, the better you will get."

"When will you teach me to cook, Mother? I want to learn to cook just like you."

"I will make a deal—when you learn a little more how to make words with those letters, I will start teaching you."

Savannah clapped, excitedly. "I can hardly wait, Mother, I want to learn to cook as good as you do."

"You will be much better than me someday, Savannah, just wait and see, and you will teach your own daughter how to cook."

"And how to write her name?"

"Yes," Alice smiled, "And how to write her name."

Savannah found herself wiping away a tear and looked across the table at Rose who was learning to write her name. R O S E, how smart Clara was to only give her four letters to learn.

"That's good, Rose, you are doing a great job."

"Rose, my name is Rose."

"Yes, you are named after a beautiful flower. It was your birth mother's favorite."

"What was her name, Momma?" she asked, even though Savannah had told her many times.

"Clara, her name was Clara, and she had beautiful blonde hair, just as you do."

Jonah smiled from across the room. He loved it when Savannah spoke of Clara to Rose. He always thought it best to teach her about her real mother. He felt as if he owed it to Clara.

"You are pretty just like she was," Savannah said, softly.

"And you are pretty, too."

"Well, thank you," Savannah laughed.

Yes, she loved days like today, when nothing else in the world mattered but here and now. But there were times her heart ached for those years long ago.

She vowed to teach Rose everything her own mother had taught her.

CHAPTER 16

Savannah brought the fresh bread out of the oven and inhaled the fragrance slowly. It smelled almost as good as springtime, when she opened the windows earlier.

John moved back to his cabin, and Savannah looked forward to life getting back to normal, almost certain John welcomed it, too, since one could only play so many games with a child who never stopped talking.

The door swung open and Jonah walked in, carrying two roosters he had killed just that morning.

"Poor Jack and George," Savannah said, sadly.

Jonah laughed. "I told you that you should not name all the chickens. Besides, these will be very tasty when we travel to help the Ingalls raise their barn tomorrow."

"Yes! I am so excited we have new neighbors in the area. I cannot wait to meet Nancy. I am so glad they have a daughter Rose's age; she will be so thrilled!"

"Do you want me to help you get these ready for frying?" Jonah set the roosters down on the table. "You know we can't have but so many roosters in the pen or they fight. I left a couple."

"No, I've watched Mother do it time after time; I already have the hot water boiling in the pot. Go and do whatever it is you men do," she shooed him out with her hand.

Jonah laughed and kissed her on the lips. "John and I are going to finish plowing the field."

"Make him be careful, Jonah, he isn't a young man like yourself."

"Don't worry, I won't allow him to do more than he can handle."

Savannah plucked the roosters and cut them up to fry for the next day's journey six miles to the east.

Jonah had discovered the new neighbors when he went hunting a couple of weeks back. Tom and Nancy Ingalls had already built their cabin before winter set in, and now they were ready to build their barn.

She hoped as time went on there would be more neighbors coming to the territory.

Savannah planned to take fried apple pies, fresh bread, fried chicken and green beans that she had dried the year before. Nancy was making things also, and together they would have a feast fit for a king.

She knew life could not get any better than this.

*****

"You can sit in the front with Jonah, John. I will sit in the back with Rose," Savannah pointed to the front of the wagon, as they prepared to leave the next morning.

"No ma'am, I will not have it, I tell ye. Ye are the lady of the house, and I respect that fact. Papa John will sit back here with this little princess," he grinned.

"I want to sit with Papa John," Rose stated.

"So be it, but don't say I didn't offer," She laughed, climbing on the wagon's seat. "Are you all as excited as I am?"

"Giddy up!" Jonah called out, putting the horse in motion. "Yes, we are so excited about all the hard work we are getting ourselves into, right, John?" he teased.

"That's right, but more excited about having me a taste of those fried pies and fried chicken we couldn't eat last night."

She giggled. "I'm sorry I made you eat stew and cornbread. I wanted to save them for today."

John winked at her as she looked behind. "Yes, ye forced us to eat stew and cornbread."

Savannah loved the way he joked, for she knew how much he loved her stew and cornbread.

"It's so nice to have another female living close, and just six miles! Do you think it will be okay if I rode occasionally to visit? I do know how to ride a horse, you know," she asked Jonah.

"It can still be dangerous for a lady out alone in these parts. Not enough people have moved in yet. Plus, there could be wild animals."

"Oh, Jonah, what is the fun in having a neighbor if I can never go visit? Besides, it's through the woods. I won't be going toward the village."

"I will make you a deal—when you want to go visit, I will go with you, how about that?"

Savannah shook her head. "Sometimes I feel that you don't trust me at all."

"I trust you; it's others I have a hard time with, and you can't negotiate with a wild animal. I want you to be safe. You and Rose are all I have."

"Hey, what about me?" John said from the back, making them all laugh.

"Sorry, John, of course you, too."

*****

Savannah clapped her hands as the Ingalls' cabin came into view. "Get ready to meet your new friend, Rose."

169

"Yay, Momma, a friend!" Rose screamed, excitedly.

Tom and Nancy heard them approaching and came outside to greet their new neighbors.

"Hello there!" Tom yelled out, as they approached the cabin.

"Whoa," Jonah yelled to the team to stop. "Hello, are you ready to build a barn?"

Tom laughed, "I don't know if I am, but my livestock are. Here, let me help you down, ma'am," Tom extended his hand to Savannah, and Jonah reached to grab Rose.

"Thank you, sir, it's nice to meet you. I am Savannah."

"How do you do, ma'am? This is my wife, Nancy."

Savannah went to Nancy and gave her a hug before laughing out loud. "You are just what I pictured, and I am so happy to have you as a neighbor."

"Hello, Savannah, I know what you mean; it will be nice having another woman around. You have a beautiful daughter. This is Grace," Nancy moved aside so Grace could be seen. She had been hiding behind her mother's skirt.

"Hello Grace," Savannah took her tiny hand. "This is Rose; she has come to play with you."

"And this is John Barge; he lives beside us and is one of the family now," Jonah introduced him, and John extended his hand to Tom.

"Pleased to meet ye, sir."

"Have you had your breakfast?" Nancy asked.

"Yes ma'am," Jonah answered, "Savannah fed us all at daybreak, but we did bring food with us for lunch."

"Rose, you run along in the house with Grace. She will show you where the toys are, and Savannah and I will unload the wagon, if you men want to get started," Nancy offered.

Savannah liked her, a take-charge kind of woman.

"Sounds like a plan," Tom agreed, giving her a kiss before leading the men toward the back side of the house.

"Now for you and me to get to know one another," Nancy winked. "I am just so happy to finally meet you. We were thrilled to find we had neighbors so close."

"Yes, I was happy when Jonah came in and told me he ran across you on one of his hunting trips. We have been in the valley three years, and you are the first neighbor so far.

Of course, John used to live about fifteen miles from us until we moved him closer."

"That was nice of you; he seems like a very nice man."

"Oh, he is, Jonah thinks of him as a father. Where do you want me to put the food?" she asked, taking the basket of fried chicken from the back.

"Here, let me help you. We can carry it in to the table. The men will be in to eat in a few hours. We can talk until then, feed them, and send them back out and talk some more," she laughed.

"Sounds good to me. I'd like that very much."

Savannah noticed that the Ingalls' cabin was a little smaller than their own, but beautiful. Nancy had done a fantastic job of turning it into a home.

"Look over there," Nancy pointed to the girls who were busy playing with a dollhouse, which Savannah guessed Tom had made for her.

"It is so nice to see Rose with a friend. She has had no one to play with but us, and I know Papa John would like the break."

"When is your next baby due?" Nancy asked.

Savannah looked at her, puzzled. "I am not with child."

"Oh, please forgive me. You have a glow about you, and I just thought..."

"Oh, it's okay. Jonah and I aren't really trying, but if it happens, it happens."

"I have watched my mother birth a lot of babies back in Kentucky; she was a midwife there."

"So, you know about birthing babies."

"Yes, I helped her a lot. I was going to do that myself, until I met Tom and his heart was set on coming to Arkansas."

"I know what you mean. I am from Georgia. Haven't seen my family there in three years. We do write letters, though, and that helps."

"I finally got a letter mailed just last week. I cannot wait to hear back," stated Nancy.

"How old are you, Nancy?" she asked, guessing she wasn't much older than herself.

"I am twenty-five. I married a little later than most. I think my father thought I was going to be an old maid."

"I am almost twenty. I married Jonah when I was sixteen."

"I thought you looked younger. So, he is older, like my Tom is to me?"

"Yes, but I hardly think of that at all."

"I know what you mean. What is age, anyway?"

*****

The men ate as if they were starved and headed back out the door. Tom already had the timber cut and ready to stack together and was grateful for more hands in the stacking process.

Savannah was proud of Jonah, always willing to lend a helping hand to those in need. He was such a smart man who knew so much about so many things. It made her proud to be his wife.

As Savannah was carrying dishes to the wash basin, she suddenly felt lightheaded and dropped the tin plate on the floor.

"Are you okay?" Nancy rushed over and slid a chair behind her, so she could sit.

"I think so, I just got a little dizzy."

"Savannah, are you sure you are not with child?"

"I don't think so."

"When is the last time you bled?"

"A few weeks ago. I have never paid much attention."

"Have you been feeling sick to your stomach at all?" Nancy asked, concerned.

"No, not until now."

"Savannah, I won't say anything, but please let me know in a couple weeks if you still have not started to bleed."

"Do you think I could actually be with child?"

"How did you feel the first time?" she looked toward Rose, and Savannah realized she thought Rose was her own.

"I did not give birth to Rose, Nancy. I have never had a child before."

"Oh, I am sorry, I did not know."

"Of course you didn't. How could you have? I guess I should have told you."

"It is none of my business, Savannah; forgive me if it seemed I was prying."

Savannah giggled. "Oh, stop, Nancy, you and I are going to be great friends; you might as well know everything."

"Then do tell," she winked, eager to hear the story.

"Jonah's first wife died during childbirth. They were our neighbors back in Georgia, in a town called Dahlonega. Talonega it was called before they changed the name. Anyway, when Rose was just three weeks old, he asked my father for my hand in marriage in exchange for his home and land, so that I could tend Rose while he traveled across the country to Arkansas."

"Wow, and how did you feel about that? Did you have a choice?"

"No, but it was okay. I had always thought a lot of Jonah, and I did not mind."

"You two seem so happy together," she smiled.

"We are now, but it wasn't always easy. Up until a few months ago, he was still very much in love with Clara, his first wife."

"Well, it is easy to see that he loves you now, so I am happy for you."

"Thank you, I am very happy."

"So, what do you think he will say if you are, in fact, with child?"

Savannah looked at Rose playing with Grace for a moment and let the question sink in. "I am not really sure. He'll be afraid, I guess."

"And how would you feel?"

"Happy, excited, afraid, too many emotions to count."

"I can understand that. So, you want a child of your own, then?"

"Oh yes, I have always wanted a child of my own."

"That is good, because it is very likely you are going to get your wish. Here, let me take that," Nancy got up and took the plate Savannah had picked up off the floor. "I will do the dishes; you just sit and talk to me."

"That doesn't seem fair. I am okay, really."

"I insist, I am used to doing dishes, but not used to having another female to talk to except Grace, and you know how that is," she laughed.

*****

Savannah was unusually quiet on the ride home with so many things going through her mind.

What if she was with child? They both knew that was bound to happen sooner or later. How would Jonah feel about it?

"Why are you so quiet this evening?" Jonah asked, after they were back home and finally alone.

"I guess I talked so much today I was tired," she managed to laugh.

"I can understand that. So how do you like Nancy?"

"She is wonderful. I like her a lot. I am so glad that I now have someone to talk to."

Jonah looked at her and made a funny face. "So, what am I? Have you not been talking me to death for three years now?"

Savannah giggled. "Yes, you are my very best friend, Jonah. I meant I now have a female friend to talk to. A woman needs another woman from time to time to share secrets with, you know?"

"So, you have secrets, do you?" he winked.

"Nothing I say seems to be coming out right tonight, Jonah. You know what I mean."

Jonah picked her up and carried her to the bed, lying down beside her. "Yes, beautiful woman, I know what you mean. I am glad you have Nancy to share all your secrets with. Just as long as you don't say anything too bad about me."

"Oh, Jonah, what on earth could I possibly say that would be bad?" she loved teasing with him.

"This is true, this is true." He leaned down and kissed her lips. He'd been waiting for this all day.

CHAPTER 17

It took five days for the Ingalls' barn to be complete.

Savannah and Rose rode over with Jonah and John three days during that time. By the last day, Nancy and Savannah had become great friends.

"What a beautiful day it is, isn't it?" Nancy asked, sitting outside with Savannah, watching Rose and Grace play in the dirt, and the men put the final touches on the barn.

"It sure is," Savannah answered. "But a sad day, also."

"Sad? Why is that?"

"Because the barn will be finished today, and I have no idea how long it will be before I see you again."

"We live merely six miles apart; jump on a horse and ride over."

"Jonah doesn't want me venturing from the house alone; he says it's still too dangerous in these parts. There are also wild animals, he says."

"Yes, Tom says the same, although I have not seen anything since we have been here. How about you?"

"No, nothing, and we have been here over three years—as far as someone dangerous. We did see a bear once pretty close to the cabin."

"They are our men and they love us. I will get Tom to bring me over in a couple of weeks for a visit."

Savannah clapped her hands as she always did when she was excited about something.

"Yes, please do. Come two weeks from today, and I will cook your dinner."

"Sounds good. I will tell Tom later tonight. Besides, I would love to see where you live."

"Not much different than your place, really."

"Every woman has a special touch. You know what they say—a man can build a house, but it takes a woman to make a home."

"I have heard Jonah say that. He always brags on me."

"Have you felt sick anymore?" Nancy thought for sure Savannah was with child.

"Yes, yesterday, and then again this morning."

"Did Jonah see you?"

"No, I am afraid to tell him. Oh, Nancy, I am so afraid I am with child and what this will do to him emotionally."

Nancy chuckled. "Well, surely he will know how it got there."

"You know what I mean. He could very well be beside himself with worry and not allow me to do anything until it is born."

"Just as he should. It is good for a husband to take care of his wife while she is with child."

"But I shall go crazy if he lets me do nothing."

Nancy patted her friend on the arm. "I am sure he will let you cook, or else he will starve."

"Nancy, you have no idea the shape he was in when we first met. He loved Clara so much. I have no idea what it would do to him if something should happen to me."

"Now listen to you talk," Nancy scolded. "That does not sound like the woman I have grown to know over the past few days. Where is your faith?"

"It does make one wonder, though."

"Have no fear, Savannah; as I told you, I have watched many babies be born and helped my mother all I could. When the time comes, get Jonah to come for me, and I will come help deliver it."

"Oh goodness, I am so glad you live close, or else I have no idea what we would have done."

"God always has a plan," Nancy said, "Always."

*****

Savannah found it hard to keep her morning sickness from Jonah, but luckily, he was always out the door right after breakfast, either hunting or working in the fields with John. Having no idea how much Savannah lay in bed between meals and felt terrible.

"Momma sick?" Rose asked, standing by the bed.

"Momma doesn't feel too good, Rose. Do you want to draw Momma a picture?"

"Yes, I want to draw a picture."

Savannah got up, remade the bed and got the supplies down for Rose to draw with.

She wondered if this baby would be a boy or a girl, and smiled, realizing it didn't matter. She loved Joseph and Mary both the same.

"I guess I better start dinner, Rose. Your Pa and Papa John will be in after while, and they will be hungry."

Nothing sounded good to her. Just the thought of food made her stomach queasy. Nancy had told her that the sickness usually went away after the third month, and she welcomed the fourth to hurry along.

If she calculated right, she would give birth sometime around Thanksgiving, right before winter. At least she would have Jonah inside more to help her.

Not long after Savannah placed a pot of beans on to cook, Jonah and John walked through the door.

"You are early," she stated.

"A bad storm is headed this way, so we decided to call it a day. Smells good, what's cooking?" Jonah asked.

"Just some beans and cornbread, but it will take a couple of hours before it's finished."

"That's okay," John said, placing his hat on the rack. "Papa John will sit right here with this princess and draw pictures, won't we?"

"Draw pictures, Papa John!" Rose yelled out, handing John a piece of paper.

Jonah walked over to Savannah and whispered in her ear. "Are you okay, my love?"

"Of course, why do you ask?"

"You looked a bit flushed when we walked in."

"I am good. I guess you just caught me by surprise. If I had known the storm was coming, I would have started dinner earlier."

"It's okay, we are in no hurry. You do so much for all of us, and I thank you for that."

Savannah finished cooking while she watched Jonah and John interact with Rose at the table. This was no time to be sick, there was just too much to do.

How would she keep this from Jonah much longer?

*****

Two weeks seemed to take forever, but at last, Savannah was excited that Tom and Nancy, along with their daughter Grace, would be arriving shortly. She had so much she wanted to tell Nancy.

She knew it was time to tell Jonah about the baby but wanted to get confirmation from someone who knew more about being with child than she did. There was no use worrying him unnecessarily.

"They are here," Jonah yelled from outside.

Savannah rushed out, with Rose right behind her.

"You'd think you are excited," chuckled Jonah.

"I am—it's been two whole weeks!"

Jonah put his arm around her as they waited for the Ingalls' wagon to come to a stop.

"Hello there," Tom said. "I could not wait to get here as these women have drove me crazy for two weeks!"

Nancy laughed as Jonah helped her from the wagon and then reached to get Grace. "I guess you can say we were a bit excited."

"Oh, me too," Savannah giggled as she hugged Nancy tight. "Come on in and eat dinner, and then we will send these men outside to do whatever it is men do."

Jonah chuckled at his excited wife. "Yes, I guess we can make ourselves useful in the barn."

*****

"Dinner was wonderful, Savannah, you outdid yourself," Tom leaned back and wiped his mouth.

"She always outdoes herself," John agreed, patting the bulge in his stomach.

"Let's us men go outside. I'll show you around the farm, Tom, and we will leave these women to talk." Jonah winked at Savannah, knowing this is what she wanted. He couldn't figure out why Savannah had been acting differently the past couple of weeks, but he hoped talking to another woman would help.

Tom pushed his chair under. "I'd love to see your farm, Jonah. Looks like you have a nice one."

"Rose, you can take Grace over to play with the toys," Savannah pointed, trying to get the girls occupied so she could talk to Nancy.

"Are you okay? You look flushed. You are still having morning sickness, aren't you?" Nancy asked.

"Oh, yes, it's been terrible. Do you think that something is wrong?"

Nancy placed her hand on Savannah's stomach and smiled when she felt the firmness of the bump. "Nothing other than you being with child."

"Are you certain? I mean are you *really* certain?"

"You have not started to bleed yet, have you?"

"No, I haven't."

"Yes, I am certain. Don't be lifting Rose; she is too heavy now. Don't be lifting anything at all that is heavy, for that matter. Drink plenty of milk; it helps build the baby's bones and teeth."

"Oh, Nancy, I have to tell Jonah."

"So, tell him. Do you want me with you when you tell him?"

"No, I will have to do this alone. I have no idea how he is going to take it."

"Well, he seems to love Rose very much, and I think he will be excited."

"And afraid. He will be afraid he will lose me, too, just like Clara."

"Then you will need to reassure him that women have babies every single day."

"It will be nice knowing you are close to help me, also."

"Yes, you can tell him that I will help when the time comes. Maybe that will give him some peace."

"I am guessing it will arrive around Thanksgiving."

"That's a great time to have a baby. I will come and stay with you a couple of days to help all I can. You will be sore for a few days and bleed heavily."

"Why am I so nervous?"

Nancy laughed, "Because it is your first child. Every woman is nervous with her first child; you are no different."

"Can I ask you something and you tell me the truth?"

"Sure, you know you can ask me anything."

"Is it very painful?" Savannah was not sure she wanted the truth.

Nancy wrapped her arms around her and hugged her tight. "From what I have seen, every woman is different. Some seem to have more pain than others. As for me, the labor wasn't easy, but it doesn't last forever, and the reward is great."

"I understand. Thank you for being here for me."

"Always, that's what friends are for."

"Please pray that Jonah receives the news well."

"I will. Do you intend to tell him later, after we leave?"

"I guess. I might as well get this over with."

*****

Savannah waved goodbye to the Ingalls as she watched them disappear. A feeling of loneliness filled her for the first time in a long time. She missed having another woman around to talk to, and today she was missing her mother more than ever. Oh, what she would give to have her close.

How would she ever get through this with a man who would be afraid he was going to lose her?

How could she reassure him God was in control when that same God did not seem to have things under control when his first baby was born?

Oh, dear Father, please help me find the words.

"As much as you have talked today, you are awfully quiet." Jonah stated, still standing beside Savannah in the front yard.

"I am sorry; I was just thinking how I would miss her."

"Savannah, they aren't far from here; it's not like you will never see her again."

"You mean like Mother?" Savannah could not help the tears. Why did she feel so emotional lately?

"Oh, Savannah, I am so sorry." Jonah pulled her close in his arms and held her. "I should not have taken you so far away from your family."

Savannah wiped her face. "It's okay, you and Rose and John are my family now. Sometimes I just miss her so bad."

"I know you do." Jonah stood for the longest and let her cry.

*****

Savannah never minded how long John stayed in the evenings, but this evening it seemed he stayed longer than usual. Maybe it was just that she wanted to talk to Jonah so badly, alone.

"Well, goodnight. I think I will turn in and leave you two alone," John grabbed his hat and headed out the door.

He always played with Rose until she fell asleep and then left, just like a good Papa John would do.

"Do you ever regret that I brought him here?" Jonah asked.

"Of course not, why would you ask such a thing? You know I love John."

"I am not sure. It's just that you have not been yourself lately, and I am worried about you."

Savannah went behind the curtain to put on her gown and lay down, waiting on Jonah to join her.

"You see," Jonah stuck his head behind the curtain.

"See what?"

"I made a statement, and you just walked off, as if you did not hear me."

"I am sorry, Jonah, please tell me again what you said."

183

Jonah got undressed and crawled under the covers beside her. "I said that you have not been yourself lately, and I am worried about you. Is there something you want to talk about? Is there something I have done wrong?"

Savannah ran her fingertips over his face. Oh, how she loved his face. "No, Jonah, you have not done anything wrong. You do everything right."

"Well then, why do I feel like I have done something wrong?"

"I am sorry; I have just been emotional lately."

"Is it because you miss your mother?"

"Maybe, but there is more to it than that."

"You seem so happy when you are around Nancy, and you change when she leaves. I know she isn't old enough to remind you of your mother. Is it just having a female around that you lack?"

"Rose is a female," she stated.

"You know what I mean, Savannah. Having a female around that is *old* enough to talk to about things."

"It is nice. I will have to admit."

"I am not a female, but I am the man that loves you. Please know you can talk to me, and I will do my best to fix whatever it is that troubles you."

"What makes you think something is troubling me?"

"Because you are not the same woman you were several weeks ago. You stay flushed and emotional, and everything seems to bother you more than usual. You cry more and…" Jonah paused. "Savannah, are you with child?"

Savannah closed her eyes, willing the words to come. "Yes, Jonah, I am carrying your child."

Jonah froze, remembering the night Clara told him she was expecting. He had been so happy until the night their baby was born, and God took her away, and his whole life changed.

"Say something, please, Jonah."

"Are you sure? Is this what you wanted to talk to Nancy about? Does she know?"

"Yes, yes and yes. Please tell me what you are feeling right now."

"I am not sure. Afraid, I guess. I mean I knew this could happen. I just don't want to lose you, Savannah. Oh, God, I would just die myself, if something happened to you."

She rubbed his face again and kissed him tenderly. "Jonah, I cannot promise nothing will happen, because I am not God. But I can say that women have babies daily, and they are still alive and well."

"I need to take you to the village and find a doctor to make sure everything is okay."

"Nancy's mother was a midwife and delivered many babies. Nancy watched her growing up and even helped her deliver a few. She said when the time comes that you can go fetch her. She is going to come and stay a couple of days and help me."

"But Savannah, it was a midwife that helped Clara. I would feel better if we got a doctor."

"Jonah, we live ten miles from town, and what if the doctor is somewhere else at the time, then what? There is no set time for a baby to arrive. Nancy is only six miles, and you know she will be there."

Jonah ran his hand through his hair and closed his eyes, thinking back to that terrible night over three years ago. He would never forget it as long as he lived, the screaming coming from the bedroom as Clara tried to deliver Rose with Nelly's help.

"Say something, Jonah."

Jonah opened his eyes and looked at her. "I know that this should be a happy time. A child is a gift from God. Every woman wants a baby, and her husband should be jumping for joy. Forgive me."

"But," Savannah encouraged him to finish.

"But it will take me a while to try to shed this fear I feel. Here I am again, Savannah, asking you for patience."

"I will give you all the time you need, for at least another six months."

"Six months? Do you think you are already that far along?"

"I am quite certain of it," Savannah took his hand and placed it on her bump. "Your child is in there, and afraid or not, it will be born around Thanksgiving."

"I love you, Savannah, and I will love our child. Our children will be blessed to have you as their mother."

CHAPTER 18

"I am excited to be going into the village, just the two of us," Savannah beamed. "It was sweet of John to offer to take care of Rose and give us this time alone. I am eager to pick out some material to make the baby a couple of gowns."

"You are even more beautiful today than you were yesterday," Jonah bragged.

Savannah laughed and placed her hand on her round belly. "Oh really? You are just too kind."

"Yes, really. You are carrying my child; why wouldn't you be beautiful?"

"It has been three months since we have seen the Ingalls. Do you think perhaps we can pay them a visit soon?"

I don't see why we can't. I would have already carried you, but I have been so busy in the fields, as I am sure Tom has also."

"Which reminds me of a few more supplies I need to get when we are at the mercantile."

"I have a surprise for you," Jonah smiled. "I think you will like it."

"Oh, I love surprises. What is it?"

"If I told you, it would not be a surprise, would it?"

"When will I find out what the surprise is?"

"As soon as we get to the village. We are going there first."

Savannah clapped her hands and placed them back in her lap. "I am so glad the morning sickness finally ended. Now I feel like I can enjoy the rest of the time I have remaining until the baby is born."

"Me too, your color has finally come back, and you seem happier."

"What do you hope for, Jonah? A son or a daughter?"

"As long as you are both healthy when it's over, I don't care."

"I have thought a lot about it. If it is a daughter, then Rose will have a little girl to play with. Of course, she will be almost four when she is born, and that is a big age difference.

And if it is a boy, then you will have a son, someone to carry on your name."

"Have you thought about names?" he asked.

"Yes, I have been thinking hard about that. How does Ruth sound for a girl, and Matthew for a boy?"

"Using Bible names, are you?"

"Yes, do you like them?"

"I do. They are both nice names."

"Wonderful! Matthew or Ruth, it is." Savannah placed her hand in Jonah's and sang Amazing Grace the rest of the way into town.

*****

Summer always seemed to bring in a lot of travelers and locals, who were buying supplies.

The village was buzzing with people everywhere today.

"I've never seen so many people," she stated, as they passed by the saloon. "Isn't the mercantile back that way?" she pointed, looking in the opposite direction.

"Yes, but remember, I told you I have a surprise for you." Jonah stopped the wagon in front of a tall building, with a sign that read Annie's Restaurant and Hotel.

"A restaurant?" she said aloud, reading the sign.

"Yes, ma'am, I am taking you on our first *real* date."

"Oh, Jonah, I have never in all my life eaten in a restaurant!"

"I figured as much. I told John to heat him and Rose some leftovers that we would be eating in town today."

"Oh, my! I am so excited," Savannah clapped.

He laughed from her excitement and helped her from the wagon. "Shall we go inside?" he asked, putting his arm out for her to take hold.

"Yes!" she took his arm and followed him in the door.

The room was crowded with people and smelled wonderful to her. So many wonderful aromas coming from the kitchen.

She looked around at all the tiny tables that were covered with white table linens, each with a small vase, filled with fresh flowers.

"I feel so out of place," she whispered.

"Well don't; you are beautiful."

"Will you be dining with us today?" a woman asked. She reminded Savannah of her past school teacher, with her silver hair pinned on top of her head.

"Yes ma'am," he answered. "A table for two, please."

"Wonderful; follow me."

They followed her to a table set for two in the corner, close to the piano. Savannah was happy it was in the corner and not the middle of the room; she already felt very uncomfortable with the size that she'd become and could feel several pairs of eyes staring at her.

Jonah pulled out her chair and she sat down.

"Thank you," he nodded to the lady who seated them.

You are welcome," she handed them each a menu. "I will be back shortly to take your order."

Savannah opened the menu and was astonished to see all the food choices. "Can we afford this?" she whispered.

He chuckled, "Yes, we can afford it. Please, choose anything you like."

"There are so many choices; how does one choose?"

"Choose as many things as you like, and don't forget dessert."

"Oh my, oh my," Savannah whispered under her breath, making Jonah laugh.

A few minutes later, the woman was back. "Have you made a decision?" she asked, politely.

Jonah nodded at Savannah to go first.

"Yes, ma'am. Could I have the meat loaf, scalloped potatoes and green beans? And could I please have peach cobbler for dessert?"

"Would you like ice cream with your pie?"

"You have ice cream?" Savannah's eyes grew wide.

"Yes ma'am, we do. Would you like a scoop on your pie?"

"Oh, yes, that sounds lovely."

"Wonderful. And for you, sir?"

"Sounds good to me, too. I'll have the same, with ice cream."

"And what would you both like to drink?"

"Do you have sarsaparilla?" Savannah asked.

"We do, and for you, sir?"

If Savannah thinks it's good, then bring us two, and I'll try it."

"Thank you both. I will get your orders as soon as I can."

Savannah watched her go back into the kitchen and whispered to Jonah. "I just realized you don't read. I am so sorry; I should have told you what was on the menu."

"Have no worries; I love meat loaf."

"I am most excited about the ice cream. I have always heard about it but have yet to try it."

"Then you are in for a treat," he smiled, taking her hand in his.

"Thank you, Jonah."

"For what?"

"For treating me like your wife."

"That is what you *are*, right?"

"Yes, but for so long I didn't *feel* like your wife."

"And that is *my* fault. I am so sorry about that."

"I understand. I am just thankful we are here, and things are better. I also want to thank you for allowing me to be me, during this," she pointed down to her round belly.

"How is that?"

"You don't smother me to death and make me lay down all the time. You allow me to continue to do the things I can do, minus the lifting," she laughed, remembering that each time she went to get anything, he was right behind her.

"I remember when Clara was with child, before it was born, she was fine. I thought everything would be okay, and there would be no complications."

"Shhhhh," Savannah placed her finger over his lips. "Let us enjoy this day, with no worries or fears for tomorrow, but enjoy today for what it is."

He smiled and kissed the top of her hand. "I love you, Savannah Bell."

"I love you more."

*****

Savannah felt stuffed as they left the restaurant. She could not remember a time when she had eaten so much at one sitting.

"That meal was incredible," she rubbed her belly. "Matthew or Ruth thank you."

"It was very good, including the sarsaparilla. How did you like the ice cream?"

191

"Oh Jonah, it was divine!"

"Wonderful, I am glad you like it. So, take my hand, my beautiful wife, and walk with me. We have another stop I want us to make."

"Another surprise?"

"Yes, but this surprise I don't wish for you to be upset about. I just would like to have peace of mind."

"Peace of mind? Oh Jonah, are you taking me to see a doctor?"

"Yes, I want him to make sure the baby is okay, and everything is going as it should be."

She smiled, realizing his fears. "Okay, I guess it will give me peace of mind also, but when the time comes, I want Nancy to deliver it, okay?"

"As long as there are no complications."

"Deal," she agreed.

Savannah followed him in the door of Doctor Terrance E. Murphy's office, located at the end of the street behind the school house.

"Might I remind you that this is also the first time I have ever been in a doctor's office?"

Then you are having a lot of firsts today," he grinned.

A balding man of about fifty walked out of the back room wearing a white coat. "Well, hello. Is there anything I can help you both with today?"

"Yes, sir. My wife is with child, and I would like for you to examine her, please. We want to make sure everything is okay with her and the baby."

"Well, certainly. How far along do you think you are?"

"I am guessing about six months, maybe seven," she answered.

"Okay, come with me to the examining room and let's have a look. Sir, you can have a seat out here; it should not take long."

Jonah sat down in a small room.

This was something he should have done with Clara, but as always, he had taken her word that everything was okay. And he knew that he would go to his grave regretting that decision.

Jonah had managed to put that terrible night out of his mind until he found out Savannah was carrying his child. Now, it seemed it was always there, especially late into the night hours when she was sleeping beside him and he held her in his arms, wondering if his days with her were numbered.

"Jonah, please leave the room!" Nelly screamed. She had never screamed at him like that, but Jonah could see she was doing everything possible for Clara, and he was only getting in her way.

"Come, Jonah," Elijah pulled him by the arm, out into the yard. "Let us go out of the way so Nelly can tend to her needs."

"Oh, Elijah, I need to go for a doctor!"

"It is too late now, Jonah, the baby will be here any moment."

Jonah paced back and forth and ran his hands through his hair, as he continued to hear his wife scream.

"Why is she screaming like that, Elijah? What is wrong? Something must be wrong!"

"Nelly screamed through childbirth, too, Jonah. It will be over soon."

Within a few minutes, the screaming stopped, and the sound of a baby's cry pierced the night air.

"We have a baby, Elijah!" Jonah said, with excitement.

"Sure sounds that way," Elijah laughed.

Nelly came to the door, crying, holding a completely covered bundle in her hand. "You have a girl," she cried.

"Is she okay?" Jonah got closer, so he could see his tiny daughter.

"Yes, Jonah," Nelly cried.

"What is wrong, Nelly? Why are you crying? Is something wrong with Clara?" Jonah could tell the tears that fell from her face were not those of excitement.

"I am so sorry, Jonah, I don't know how to tell you this, but Clara has passed!"

"What?" Jonah screamed, rushing to her bedside. "Wake up, Clara, wake up!" he shook her lifeless body.

"I'm so sorry, Jonah," he heard Elijah say from behind him. "I am so very sorry."

For as long as Jonah lived, he would never forget the look on Clara's face, so pale, yet peaceful. The room smelled of blood, and it was everywhere.

"Jonah, are you okay?" Savannah asked, which brought him back to the moment.

Jonah stood. "Yes, yes, I am okay, how about you?"

"I will let Doctor Murphy tell you himself."

Doctor Murphy took Jonah's hand in his as he spoke. Jonah could tell he was a kind man, who genuinely cared for his patients.

"Your wife has told me about the loss of your first wife during childbirth. I am terribly sorry for your loss, sir. Unfortunately, at times women do pass. Sometimes even before they deliver, so I am glad it was after your daughter was born. She possibly had heart problems that you did not know about. Many times, that is the case.

"However, after examining Savannah, I find her heart to be strong and the baby's heart to be strong. Everything seems to be just as it should be at this stage."

"Thank you, sir, that is good to know." He felt as if a load had been lifted off his shoulders.

"Savannah tells me that she has someone who is experienced to help her deliver this baby. There is nothing hard about bringing a baby into the world. She will know when the time is close, and you can go get her help. If you should need me, please let me know."

*****

It made Savannah happy to know their baby was doing well, and she prayed it would also give Jonah peace, at least for a while.

Jonah had left her in the mercantile while he went for a haircut.

"Good day to you," Savannah heard a familiar voice.

Savannah turned to see the woman from the saloon standing behind her.

"It looks like you have grown a bit since the last time we spoke," she laughed, looking at her rounding belly.

Savannah rubbed her belly and smiled. "Yes, it looks like that handsome man and I are with child."

"I want to apologize for making you feel beneath me. I have been watching and waiting for you to come back into the village, so I could say just that."

"Why would you apologize to me?"

"Because I can tell that I offended you." The woman stuck out her hand, trying to make peace. "I don't think I have ever properly introduced myself. My name is Dottie, and you might be...?"

Savannah took her hand. "Savannah. Savannah Bell."

"It's nice to meet you, Savannah. I want to say something to you that might shock you."

"Nothing you say to me at this point will shock me, Dottie."

Dottie laughed. "I guess I asked for that. The truth is, Savannah, I envy your life. You have a life I could never have. A fine husband, a daughter, and another on the way. And it is clear to see that handsome man loves you with all his heart. That is something, Savannah, I will never have. Men don't come to town and seek me out to love, at least not more than one night."

"If that be the case, Dottie, then it is because that is what they expect from you."

Dottie stood in silence a moment before smiling. "Maybe you are right. You are wise beyond your years, Savannah."

"It has been a pleasure speaking to you, Dottie, and I thank you for apologizing. Now if you don't mind, I have some material to pick out before Jonah gets here."

CHAPTER 19

"I hope you are not upset with me," Savannah reached over to take Jonah's hand on their ride home. Darkness was fast approaching, and he had hardly said a word to her in quite some time.

"Why would you think that I was upset?"

"Because you haven't spoken to me but a few words since we left the village."

"Savannah, a man does not need to rattle like a woman to prove everything is okay. Sometimes it is nice just to be silent and think."

"I'm sorry I am a rattle box."

"I love the fact that you are a rattle box; it does not bother me at all."

"Are you upset that I told Doctor Murphy about Clara?"

"No. I somewhat guessed you would."

"I wanted him to know why you were so concerned, and I wanted him to give you peace."

"It did, thank you."

"Really? I mean you are no longer worried about me?"

"I would lie if I said I was not worried. Truth is, I will probably be worried until the baby comes and you are okay afterwards."

"I could tell you were in deep thought about something, and I wasn't sure what it was. I will no longer pry."

He laughed out loud. "Oh yes, you will, because that is what makes you, you. And I love that about you."

Savannah giggled. "Good, because I knew it was going to be hard not to, but I was going to give it my best try."

"If you want to know what is on my mind, I will tell you. I keep thinking about what Doctor Murphy said about Clara, that it could have possibly been her heart. And If I had taken her to the doctor, would that have changed anything? I tried my best to get her to go to the doctor, but she insisted that she was healthy."

"Jonah, don't beat yourself up; it is not your fault."

"I am sure you get tired of me talking about Clara all the time. I am sorry if that hurts you."

"I know how much you loved her, but I also know how much you love me, so it does not upset me. I am glad you feel that you can talk to me about the things of your heart."

"Thank you for saying that. You are my very best friend, Savannah. God made you special."

She smiled. He always said the nicest things.

*****

Dearest Mother,

As I sit and write you this letter, I am watching Rose play in the creek and Jonah and John gather vegetables in the field. We have a nice crop this year, and Jonah will leave in the morning to market with some, and I will put up the rest for winter.

Jonah and John have been working on an underground storage not far from the house, so that we can store things through the harsh winter. It will also be a good place that we can all go should there be a bad storm. Sometimes the storms here are frightening.

Mother, I hope you are sitting down as you read this, for I have a bit of news that I thought might please you. I guess I should have written this by now.

*I am with child and have been for the past six months.
The last letter I wrote, I was with child but did not know it
at the time.*

You will have another grandchild sometime in November.

*Jonah took me to see a doctor and he says that everything
is okay, and the baby and I are healthy.*

*Jonah is still worried, as he lost Clara during childbirth,
so I understand. I am sure any man would be worried that
had already gone through such a loss.*

*I have a wonderful neighbor, named Nancy, that has
experience delivering babies. Jonah is going to fetch her when
the time comes.*

*Please tell everyone I said hello and that I love them all
very much.*

*And please continue to pray for us and for a healthy
baby. I am doing fine, and feel great, so please do not
worry.*

*I wish you were here with me. There are times I cry for
no reason, but Nancy says that is to be expected when you are
carrying a child.*

*I am happy, and glad to be having a baby. Jonah is the
kindest man in the world and treats me so good. I know that
makes you happy to hear that.*

Your daughter,
Savannah.

*****

Savannah placed the letter in the envelope and stuck it in
her pocket, for Jonah to take to the post office when he went to
market, knowing by the time her mother received the letter and
wrote back, the baby would already be born.

She'd been feeling the baby kick for a while. It helped her to know that everything was okay, and the baby was growing and healthy.

"Come here, Rose. Come feel your brother or sister."

Rose got out of the creek and ran over. Savannah took her small hand and placed it where she felt movement. Rose's eyes grew wide as she felt the movement for the first time.

"That feels funny," she laughed.

"It will not be long now, and the baby will be born."

"Does it hurt, Momma?"

"No, it does not hurt when it kicks."

"It is going to play with me."

"Yes, it will play with you when it learns to walk and talk. At first it will be very tiny, just like your doll, and we will have to be very careful."

"Can I hold it?"

"Of course you can, as long as you are sitting down. I will let you hold it. It is going to love you very much."

"Yay!" Rose jumped up and down.

Savannah loved watching her grow. At three and a half, she acted much older than her age. Hearing a wagon approach, Savannah turned to see the Ingalls rounding the corner toward their home.

"Nancy!" Savannah waved. It had been much too long since she'd seen her friend, and she was excited to see her. What a nice surprise.

"Come, Rose, Grace is here to play with you."

"Yay, Grace is here!" Rose ran toward the wagon.

"It is so good to see you all," Savannah clapped, as the wagon came to a stop. "Jonah was going to take me to visit a few days ago, but you can see he never has time," she pointed to the field.

"It is good to see you, too. I made Tom bring us over; I could not wait any longer. You look like you have blossomed," she smiled.

Savannah turned to the side, so Nancy could get a better view. "A little bit," she teased.

Tom hugged Savannah and helped the women down from the wagon. "I think I will go help the men and let you girls have your privacy."

Nancy hugged Savannah tight and felt her belly. "I'm sure you're feeling it kick?"

"Yes, at first it felt like I swallowed a butterfly."

"Oh, yes, I remember that well. Let's get this food and take it inside," Nancy reached for a basket in the back.

"If I had known you were coming, I would have cooked for you."

"I don't expect you to cook for me. I wanted to cook for you, my friend. I remember how it was to be in your condition."

They carried in the food and sat down at the table to talk.

"Rose, take Grace over to play after you put on some dry clothes."

Rose ran to the trunk and got out a dress to put on. "Okay, Momma."

"They grow fast, don't they?" Nancy smiled, watching their girls. "Much too fast. It seems like yesterday we were riding across the country, and I was feeding her goat's milk with a wooden spoon."

"She is a blessed little girl to have you as her momma."

"I am the one who is blessed," Savannah beamed. "And I am so glad you decided to come and see me today."

"It has been much too long. I wanted to come and check on you. You seem as though you are doing good and you look great. When did the morning sickness end?"

"After the third month, just as you said."

"Good. So, is Jonah being terribly protective?"

"Somewhat, but not as bad as I thought he would be. He took me to see a doctor in the village."

"Is that so? How did that go?"

"Doctor Murphy said the baby and I are doing well."

"And did that give Jonah peace?"

"A little, but he still has nightmares over what happened before. He wakes up during the night sometimes. I guess me being with child triggered it."

Nancy patted her hand. "It will be over soon, and things will be back to normal."

"And we will have a little one," Savannah smiled. "I can hardly wait to meet it."

"Are you hoping for a girl or a boy?"

"I doesn't really matter; I will love anything God blesses me with."

"That's the way I felt when I was carrying Grace. I think Tom secretly hoped for a boy, but to just look at them, they are wonderful together. She is certainly Daddy's girl."

"So, what have you been up to?" Savannah wanted to hear everything.

"Putting up food, as I am sure you have, too. And doing a bit of sewing. In fact, I brought you over some nightgowns for the baby and a new dress for Rose. I will have to get it out of the wagon before we leave."

"That is so kind of you. I am sure they are beautiful, thank you."

"I am sure the men will be in soon. Let me get the food on the table and have it ready."

"I can help with that," Savannah got up and Nancy pushed her gently back down.

"You could, but you won't. I am here to pamper you today, my friend. Just sit back and enjoy yourself."

*****

Savannah was tired by the time she lay down that evening. The day had turned into the most wonderful day spent with her friend, while the men gathered vegetables, and even Tom helped them.

She could hear John and Jonah talking on the other side of the curtain and laughed to herself, remembering when she told Jonah that she would never go to bed before they did.

Lately, it was all she could do to stay up much past dark. Jonah and John always let her lie down early, and they talked quietly until Rose fell asleep.

"That was a nice crop we got in today," John said.

"Yes, God has blessed us even more than last year's crop. Would you mind staying here tomorrow and letting me go into town? I don't want to leave Savannah alone with her being so far along."

"Sure, I don't mind. Would ye like for me to take the crop to market and ye stay?" John offered.

"No, it's okay, you've had a long, hard week. I will take it. You stay and rest. I feel like I ask too much of you."

John laughed. "Ye ask *nothing* of me, Jonah, I just jump in and roll my sleeves up and help, as I should."

"And I do appreciate that."

"And I appreciate ye and Savannah taking me in and treating me like family."

"You *are* family, John, you know that."

John smiled, as he rocked Rose. "And ye let me be this one's Papa John. That means a lot to me."

"And you will be the next little one's Papa John also."

"Ye know everything is going to be all right, don't ye, Jonah?" John remembered well their conversation and knew he must be beside himself with worry.

"Savannah keeps telling me it will, and I have to trust that. I feel somewhat better since the doctor checked her and the baby."

"I was not blessed with a child, Jonah, so I don't know what ye going through, but I pray for ye nightly that ye will find peace."

"I have been having nightmares, horrible dreams."

"Do ye want to talk about it?"

"I keep dreaming that I am back in Georgia, and it is the night Clara screamed in pain. And when Nelly tells me she has passed, I run in and it's not Clara in the bed, but Savannah."

John placed his hand on Jonah's arm. "Satan is trying to get to you. Try not to let him. Stay positive and prayed up."

Jonah chuckled. "It wasn't so long ago I stopped praying."

"But ye do now; I know ye do."

"Yes, it seems I pray all the time."

"That is good, for one can never be too close to God. He knows how ye feel, and He will comfort ye."

"If it wasn't for Savannah's faith, I am not sure I would ever be able to trust in God again."

"Savannah is a good woman, one of the best I ever seen. She's so much like my Martha. My Martha had faith like that. Do ye know what they say about a man and a woman?"

"What is that?"

"A man is the head, but a woman is the neck."

Jonah nodded in agreement. "And you can't turn a head without a neck."

Savannah smiled and snuggled deeper under the quilt. It would be a while before Jonah came to bed, and she couldn't stay awake any longer.

CHAPTER 20

I felt the first signs of fall this morning, and even though I usually dread seeing summer end, I find myself giddy over it this year.

With fall, it means our little one is close to being born.

I have thought about it a hundred times and what it will be like. I try not to allow myself to get caught up in the wonder, or it shall drive me mad.

I find myself wondering about so much these days. Will it be Matthew or Ruth? Will Jonah love it as much as he does Rose?

Will Rose be jealous when it arrives because she no longer gets all the attention, especially since she knows I am not her birth mother?

I will make a point to tell her how much I love her each day, as much as I do the baby.

Will I be able to get through the pain of childbirth, and will there be complications that Nancy cannot handle?

But why would I think that, Lord, why would that ever even cross my mind? I did not even know Clara well, and yet lately I cannot get her off my mind.

Perhaps it is because of the dreams that plague Jonah, as he wakes up each night covered in sweat and tells me it's nothing. But now I know what his dream is, for I overheard him tell John.

Satan tries to invade my mind, reminding me, that should something happen, Jonah would be left alone, and would that be the last straw, that took away his belief in God forever?

Oh Lord, please calm my fears, for I cannot talk to Jonah about this. I can only talk to you.

*****

Jonah put the finishing touches on the cradle and stood back to admire it. He had left Rose's cradle back in Georgia, for it was much too big to carry in the wagon.

He knew the new cradle was some of his best work, and he hoped Savannah liked it.

"Savannah," he called to her, as she was gathering clothes off the line.

"Yes, Jonah?" she looked toward the barn and saw him standing at the door—so handsome he was.

"Can you come here a moment? I have something to show you."

Savannah left the basket and started toward the barn, wondering what it was he wanted to show her. Ever since the barn had been built, she had only entered it a few times, as she felt it was her place in the house—cleaning, cooking and taking care of Rose.

"I told you I'd gather the clothes in just a bit. I don't want you carrying anything too heavy," Jonah scolded.

Savannah smiled and placed her hands on the small of her back. "Did you call me out here to get on to me, or do you *really* have something to show me?"

Jonah took her hand and led her into the barn to the cradle. "How do you like it?"

Savannah clapped her hands and screamed with joy, "Oh, Jonah, it is beautiful! I love it!"

"I have Nancy working on the padding; she will bring it the day she comes to deliver the baby."

"I will have to thank her. How long have you been working on this?"

"Not long. I wanted to get it finished before the baby came. I know we will need a place to lay it while it sleeps."

Savannah kissed him tenderly and pulled him in a tight embrace. "I love you, Jonah. Thank you for loving me and our baby the way you do. I cannot wait until we can stop calling the baby an it, and start calling it he or she."

"Only a couple more weeks, right?"

Savannah took his hand and placed it on her hard stomach. "Or sooner. It doesn't move as much as it used to, and I feel the time is getting close."

"Do you think something is wrong?" he worried.

"No, Nancy said when it gets close, they get positioned and don't move as much. I guess it doesn't have as much room to move around."

"That makes sense. Do you think we need to ride in to Doctor Murphy's office and let him check, just to be sure?"

"No, I honestly don't think I could make the ride, right now, with all the bumps. I think everything is okay."

Jonah nodded his head in agreement, knowing there was nothing left to do except pray.

"Let me get this moved into the house and placed where you want it."

"Let's put it beside the bed for now. It will sleep close for a few months."

"Yes. I will take it in now, and then be back to carry in the clothes."

Savannah loved this man more than life itself. How did she ever get so lucky?

*****

"Noooooo!" Jonah screamed out in his sleep.

"Jonah, it's okay," Savannah, whispered. "Wake up, you are just having a bad dream."

"Oh, Savannah, come and let me hold you."

"Are you okay?"

"It's the same dream I keep having. I am hoping it will end after the baby comes."

"Is it about Clara?" Savannah did not wish to tell him she already knew and hoped he would talk to her about it himself.

"Yes, or at least it starts as Clara, and then it's you. Oh, Savannah, I will be a basket case when you start to deliver."

"If it helps, you can take Rose and go to John's cabin."

"I've already told John when it happens to take Rose and go to his cabin, but as for me, I don't plan to leave your side."

"My father was not in the room when Joseph and Mary were born."

"As I said, I do not intend to leave your side for even a moment."

"I am sorry this is putting such stress on you."

"It isn't your fault, Savannah. You see, I left Clara, and she died. I don't plan to leave you; I hope you and Nancy are okay with that."

"It is okay with me if you stay."

"I am sorry I woke you. Can I hold you while you go back to sleep?"

"I would like that very much."

*****

Jonah leaned against the tree with his rifle, waiting to carry home fresh meat. It had been a while since he had carried home game, and with winter on its way, he wanted to prepare. He also knew the baby would be here any day, and he did not plan on hunting much for a few weeks afterward. He planned to help with the baby as much as he could.

He did not like to venture too far from home these days, as Savannah had gotten much slower and had swelling in her hands and feet. If she was anything like Clara, it was just a matter of time.

Oh, how he hated to even think about it. He hoped she was *nothing* like Clara, when it came to having their baby.

He feared that if something was wrong, Nancy wouldn't know what to do, just as Nelly had not. He had often wondered if there could have been anything she could have done different? Would Clara still have died, even if a doctor had been present?

Oh Lord, please forgive me for ever doubting You.

I will never understand Your ways, but Your ways are not for me to question.

Thank You, for bringing Savannah into my life, for she is the best part of me.

Lord, I ask if You should decide You need her, then please take me instead.

I know I could not bear it if I lost her, and she would have John and Tom to help her, but I would never love another woman, for as long as I live.

With her death, I would also die.

Forgive me, as I know I shouldn't feel this way, but I am merely human, and as much as I want to have the faith she has, I know in my heart I don't.

I'm telling You this now, so You don't test me later.

I can just hear Savannah say, God doesn't test us, but sometimes I feel as if You do, and I know if that be the case, then I seem to always fail miserably.

I am but a humble man, here now, asking You to please watch over her and protect her and keep her safe.

Two shots rang out close to the house, causing Jonah to jump to his feet and take off running, knowing it was John telling him the time had come.

They had talked about what they would do, should she go into labor while he was in the field or away from the house many times.

John was standing outside and already had his horse waiting on him.

"Her water broke, and she is going into labor; I know you are a better rider than me, hurry."

Jonah jumped on his horse and took off, calling behind him, "Stay close to her; we will be right back."

I need You now, Lord. I need You to ease her pain and protect her.

Jonah rode hard through the woods to the Ingalls house. It was almost dusk, and he knew he had to hurry to get Nancy back before the world went black.

Finally, he saw the house coming into view and Tom outside stacking firewood.

"Tell Nancy it's time!" he screamed out, still a few feet from the house.

Tom took off inside to get Nancy, and within minutes, Nancy jumped on the back of Jonah's horse with him.

"I love you Tom, I'll be back in a few days," she called, as they took off.

"How is she?" Nancy yelled, holding on tight.

"I don't know. I was hunting, and John signaled me to let me know her water had broke. She was in labor. I do hope she is okay."

"I am sure she is fine; we just need to remember to stay calm for her sake."

John was out in the yard waiting for their return. "She is in bed waiting on you. I am going to take Rose and go to my cabin."

"Thank you," Jonah said, jumping off the horse and helping Nancy down.

Nancy hurried into the house with Jonah on her heels.

"How are you doing?" she asked.

Savannah had already put on the pot of water and had clean linens ready. "So far so good, just a few minor contractions."

"How long ago was it your water broke?"

"Two hours ago, give or take."

"It could take a while for the contractions to get stronger. Let me check to see how far you have dilated. Jonah, do you want to stay or go to John's cabin? I can come get you when it's here."

"I'm staying," Jonah pulled a chair beside Savannah and took her hand.

Nancy lifted her legs and smiled, "I see you already have your underwear off and ready."

"But of course, I follow instructions well."

Jonah was not in the room when Nelly had checked Clara, so this was new to him. So far this seemed as if it would be a breeze. Maybe God had heard his prayer.

"You are about an eight now, Savannah. Let me know when the contractions get stronger."

"You will be the first to, Ahhhhhhhh," she yelled out, squeezing Jonah's hand hard.

"Okay, Savannah, when a contraction hits, I want you to breathe like this," Nancy took three short breaths, twice. "Breathe in slow through your nose and let it out your mouth, as if you are panting like a dog. Jonah, I need you to get me some sewing thread and a very sharp knife."

"I have it on the table and ready," Savannah answered.

"Good girl."

"Why do you need a knife?" Jonah looked worried.

"To cut the cord. Have no worries, I need you to stay calm."

"That is easy for you to say," he said under his breath.

"Ahhhhhhhh, it hurts!" Savannah yelled again.

"Yes, Savannah, it does hurt, sweetie. The baby's head was starting to crown. I could feel it when I checked you. Just don't push until I tell you to."

"Are you sure everything is all right? Should I go get the doctor?"

"Everything is just as it should be, so far. Besides, it's dark and he is ten miles away, if he is even there right now. The baby will be here before you have a chance to get back."

Savannah let out another scream that sent chills down Jonah's spine.

"Just a few minutes ago she was fine," Jonah reminded Nancy.

"Jonah, why don't you go pace?"

"I'll stop, but I am not leaving her side."

Nancy smiled and nodded.

Half an hour passed, with the contractions coming every three minutes. Nancy nodded and smiled, as she checked her the second time.

"Okay, it is about time to push; that went much faster than I thought." Nancy removed the quilt and got Savannah positioned.

"Ouch!" Savannah cried. "It hurts so bad, Nancy. I don't think I can do this!"

"Yes, you can, Savannah, just keep breathing like I showed you."

"But. It. Hurts!" Savannah screamed out, again.

"All right, Daddy, I need you to get close beside her and pull her knees back like this. If you insist on staying, you can help me."

"I'll do my best," he said and did as he was told.

"Okay, Savannah, when I say push, I want you to push with all that you have. Push with your bottom."

"Is this the way?" Jonah asked, holding her knees back.

"That is perfect."

"Ahhhhhhh, it's hurting so bad! I can't take it!" she cried.

"Push, Savannah, push."

Savannah pushed with all she had, then stopped to take a breath.

"That's good, you are doing great! Take a deep breath, hold it, and push again. One, two, three, and push!"

Savannah did as she was told and pushed again. And again, she stopped to breathe. "I am sorry, I can't.... hold my breath..... that long.... Ahhhhhhh, oh God, please help me," she screamed.

Jonah looked at Nancy briefly, with worry on his face.

Nancy winked. "Hang in there, Daddy. And again, Savannah, on the count of three, deep breath and hold it. One, two, three, and push!"

Savannah pushed hard and out came the baby's head. Jonah gasped.

"It's coming, Savannah—push again, push really hard this time. One, two, three, and push hard!"

"Ahhhhhhhhhhh," Savannah pushed hard, and out came the baby with a loud pop.

"Way to go, Savannah," Nancy laughed through tears. "You both have a beautiful baby boy."

"Oh my gosh," Savannah cried. "Is he okay?"

Nancy quickly cleaned the mucus out of his nose and mouth, held him upside down by his feet and gave him a quick slap on the bottom to get him to take his first real breath. The baby cried loudly.

"I'd say he is just fine." Nancy took the thread and tied the umbilical cord tight before cutting it with the knife.

"He is beautiful," Jonah cried.

"Here Daddy, I need you to take him to the table and clean him up good, and let me finish with Savannah."

"Finish?" he was confused.

"Yes, we still have an afterbirth to deliver. Don't worry, this is natural. Savannah is doing fine, aren't you, Savannah?"

Savannah laughed. "Yes, I am wonderful. Thank you so much, Nancy."

"It's not over yet, Sweetie, you can thank me later." Nancy motioned Jonah away and closed the curtain off from the main room.

Jonah carried his newborn son to the table and lay him on a blanket and took warm rags and wiped him clean. "You are simply amazing," he said to him.

Jonah put on a nappie and wrapped him in a clean blanket Savannah had made, and carried him to the rocker.

"Hello, Matthew," he said, looking at his little hands and counting his fingers.

"Okay, you can come back now and bring that baby to its momma; we are all done and cleaned up here."

Jonah walked to the bed and placed Matthew in Savannah's arms. "He's perfect, just like his mother."

She looked down upon his tiny face. "And he is handsome just like his father. Oh, Jonah, isn't he beautiful?"

Jonah felt as if the floodgates had opened and all his pent-up emotions came pouring out. All he could do was fall back in the chair and cry.

Nancy walked over to him and put her arms around him from behind. "Are you okay, Daddy?"

"I am just so grateful it is over, and everyone is okay."

Savannah looked at Nancy and smiled, so glad that he was letting it all go.

"I am going to get John and Rose; I know they will want to see the baby. I will leave you two alone for a little bit." Nancy left the house.

"I love you, Jonah, thank you for not leaving me."

"I wouldn't have left you if you had wanted me to."

"Maybe now, when we have our third child, you won't be so nervous."

Jonah laughed, "You are already thinking about our third child when you just gave birth to our second?"

"Well, you just never know what God plans for us. Who knows, we may have five or six."

Jonah put his hands on his chest. "Oh, no, stop me now!" he joked.

"I had no idea how bad childbirth was, Jonah."

"And here you are already talking about another one."

"But just look at him. He is so adorable and worth every ounce of pain."

Jonah got close and looked at him again. "Yes, he is. He is just perfect."

Within a few minutes, Nancy came back in with John and Rose.

"I wanna see," Rose screamed.

John lifted her up and let her look at her new baby brother. "He is a fine boy," John said through tears.

"Can I hold him?" Rose asked.

"Let's wait until tomorrow, sweet girl," Nancy answered. Your momma is tired, and she still has to feed your little brother.

"Okay," Rose said, sadly.

"Savannah laughed, "I promise you, Miss Rose, you are going to get to hold him all you want and play with him. So, don't be sad."

"Thank you for taking care of her for a while," Jonah said to John.

"Anytime; it's my pleasure."

"Okay, let's give this little momma some privacy and let her feed her new son, so she can get some rest. She has had a hard evening," Nancy reminded everyone.

John carried Rose to the other side of the curtain, and Jonah gave Savannah a kiss.

"I will sleep on the bed roll a couple of nights and give you some space."

"No sir, you won't. You made this bed big enough for two of us. I will put Matthew in his beautiful cradle as soon as I have fed him. You don't have to leave."

"Never, I will never leave. I am just going to talk to John for a bit. I will be right back."

Savannah looked at Nancy and motioned for her to come closer. "I love you, my friend. I could not have done it without you. I am sorry I was such a wimp."

"Who are you kidding? You were one of the strongest patients I've ever seen. You did great."

"You are just saying that," she giggled.

"No, I mean it. You did great. And I love you, too. Now feed that little bundle and get some rest. I will stay with you a couple of days and cook for these men and let you rest, but I am afraid Tom and Grace may be over tomorrow to see the new addition," Nancy winked and left her alone.

Savannah kissed Matthew on the top of the head.

Momma loves you, little man. Momma loves you so very much.

CHAPTER 21

Nancy stayed three days before going home. She wanted to help Savannah as much as she could. She remembered so well how hard it was, those first few days after giving birth to Grace.

On the last day, Nancy cooked a turkey Jonah had shot, and they all gathered together for a Thanksgiving feast. All seven of them gathered around the table, with the little bundle sleeping in his cradle.

"I could never thank you enough for staying so long, Nancy," Savannah said.

"It was my pleasure. I wanted to stay long enough to help you with Thanksgiving also, and the selfish side of me wanted us all together. I knew Tom and Grace would be here, if they come to get me," she laughed.

"Thanks for letting her stay with us so long," Jonah said to Tom. "We could never have done it without her. She was a champ, better than any doctor around."

"I wouldn't go that far," Nancy laughed.

"Well, I have to admit, we are happy to get her back. I am not cut out to be a mother," Tom joked.

"You and me both," agreed Jonah.

John got up from the table and looked out the window. "I thought I saw snow falling," he said.

"No way, this early?" Tom got up to look out. "Well, I hate to cut this party short, but we better help clean up and be on our way before it gets any worse."

"I can clean up; you go on if you want," Savannah got up from the table to clear the dishes and Nancy took it out of her hands.

"Not on my time. Sit, let me wait on you once more before I go."

Savannah sat down and sighed. "You are spoiling me."

"I probably won't see you again until springtime, so enjoy it while you can."

Savannah hated seeing Nancy leave again; the two of them had gotten close since they met, especially in the last few days.

Nancy had taken care of Rose and done all the cooking and cleaning, while she had done nothing but hold and feed Matthew. She vowed to do the same for her, should she ever need to.

*****

Winter here, by far, is my least favorite season.

At least being closed up for a while is much better than it used to be when we first came to the valley.

Jonah is the most wonderful loving husband a woman could ever have asked for, and such a great father to both Rose and Matthew.

He has had no trouble bonding this time. In fact, he loves holding him. He always makes a point to hold Rose first and then Matthew. I love him for that.

Rose loves her little brother. She thinks it is great to be a big sister and talks to him all the time telling him just what she plans to do with him when he is old enough to walk and to talk.

Christmas was wonderful this year and the New Year is in two days. It is so hard to believe it will be 1836. Where does the time go?

I am looking forward to springtime and seeing Nancy and Tom and Grace.

Rose talks about Grace all the time and longs to see her and play with her since her little brother does nothing yet but eat and sleep and cry.

I will never regret coming here with Jonah. I could not picture myself being anyone else's wife, or not being Rose or Matthew's mother.

Life is good, and I am truly grateful.

Savannah lay down her paper and picked up her little bundle, who was now awake and eager to be fed. Everyone else was sleeping.

Jonah had stopped having nightmares, and she was thrilled that he was once again at peace.

Savannah offered Matthew her breast, and he latched on hungrily. This was her favorite time of day, when the whole world seemed to be sleeping except her.

Her time alone, with her son, and she wondered how Mary felt when she held baby Jesus, knowing that He was not only hers but was the true son of God, who would one day die for us all.

*****

Savannah awoke to the sound of birds singing. What a glorious sound, for it meant warmer weather was on its way and no more snow for at least a few months.

"Can I play in the water?" Rose asked, wanting to play in the creek.

Savannah laughed. "The water is still too cold, Rose. You will have to wait a couple more months. Just because the snow is gone doesn't mean it is summer yet."

Jonah and John left early to go into the village for seed to be planted as soon as they plowed the ground.

She could hardly wait for their return, as she eagerly awaited a letter from her mother. It had been so long since she had received one and knew by now her mother would know she had a baby.

After feeding Matthew and laying him down to nap, Savannah busied herself cleaning. Springtime had a way of making her want to make things clean and fresh, and besides, it helped her pass the time until the men came home, hopefully with her letter.

By the time Jonah and John returned that evening, the house was spotless, and a dinner of eggs, ham and homemade biscuits was on the table.

Jonah came through the door carrying a new doll for Rose, and she jumped up and down with excitement. "She is pretty, Pa."

"I thought you would like her. And this is yours," he said, handing Savannah a new journal.

"Oh, thank you, Jonah; I needed this more than you know."

"I know, I see you writing all the time."

"I'd still love to teach you how to read and write."

"As long as I have you reading to me, there is no need," he winked. "I also got you this," he said as he brought out several yards of different colored materials.

"What pretty colors, thank you. Did I happen to get a letter?"

"Oh, no, John, we forgot to stop at the post office."

"Well, goodness, Jonah, we sure did," John went along with him.

"Jonah Bell, you better not have forgotten to have gone to the post office. You took a letter to mail for me today. Please tell me you are only joking with me."

Jonah laughed and reached into his pocket to get her letter.

Savannah took it and kissed it and stuck it in her pocket.

"You aren't going to read it?" John asked.

Jonah shook his head. "She never reads it until she is alone; it's her tradition."

"He is right," she agreed. "I figure I waited this long, what is a little bit longer? I don't want any interruptions."

"Makes perfectly good sense to me," John laughed. "Boy, something sure smells good."

"Then sit down and let's eat. I have had it ready for a bit," Savannah motioned, taking off the cloth she had spread over the food.

"Yes, oh yes, I am one lucky man," Jonah smiled. "One lucky man, indeed."

*****

After everyone was sleeping and Matthew was fed, Savannah opened her letter. It had been a long day, but there was no way she was finding sleep until she read the letter she had waited so long to receive.

Dear Savannah,

I cried from happiness when I received your letter. My baby, about to have a child of her own. I am just so happy for you.

I have always said you never know how much I love you, until you have your own child, and I know by the time you receive my letter, you will already know.

A mother's love has no limits.

Sure, a father loves a child, but he will never understand what it is like to carry one inside you for nine months and feel it grow and kick. There is no other bond like it. Now I cannot wait until your next letter to find out if I have a grandson or another granddaughter and what you named it.

Your father has been under the weather as of late and Joseph has picked up the slack. It amazes me what all he can do for a young boy his age. He has grown so much over the past four years since you have been gone, and he looks forward to your letters every bit as much as I do.

Thank you also, for writing Mary her own letters. At almost six, she is learning to read, and I do want her to know her older sister and what is going on in her life.

As for me, I am still sewing and seem to have a long stack now I am trying to get finished for everyone in town. It seems word has gotten out and I have more than I can do. But of course, I thank God, for it pays well.

I am starting to teach Mary how to sew, just as I did you. I am letting her do small things, like darning the socks people send me. She loves having a penny to spend at the store.

I have also started baking cakes and pies and selling those also.

With your father being quite a bit older than me, I want to make sure we will be okay should something ever happen.

Of course, I did not say that for you to worry. We are all doing fine and missing you terribly.

Please tell Jonah, Rose, and Papa John I said hello.

I love you so very much,

Mother.

Savannah wiped her tears and folded her letter. The hardest part of being here was missing the people there. It had taken them several weeks to travel from Dahlonega to Arkansas by wagon, and she knew the likelihood of seeing her mother again was slim.

She stood and placed the letter into the beautiful box Jonah had made her and closed the lid slowly as not to wake Rose or Matthew and tiptoed quietly to bed.

*****

The summer breeze felt wonderful under the huge oak tree.

Rose played in the creek and Matthew played on a blanket on the soft grass. He was now turning over and starting to scoot to get to where he wanted to go.

She had been with Jonah over four years now, and other than missing her Georgia family, she could not be happier.

She had written her mother not long ago, telling her of her grandson and that his name was Matthew. And just two weeks ago had got the news of her father's passing.

It felt strange to Savannah that it had not affected her more than it did. She'd never been that close to her father; she only felt sorry for her mother who would now have to do it alone.

Of course, from her mother's last letter, she was already doing it on her own, and had been for a while now, with her sewing and baking, and of course Joseph helping so much for his age.

Maybe now that her father had passed, she hoped to one day talk her family into taking a stagecoach and coming to visit.

There had also been talk of a railway coming in that would take people much faster than stagecoach or wagon. Who knows, maybe there was hope to see her mother and siblings, after all.

Savannah smiled at Matthew and had the most marvelous idea. What if she talked her mother into coming to Arkansas to live? If Jonah could build John a cabin, maybe he would build her mother one, too.

She knew that her mother would love Nancy, and of course Nancy would love her mother. Yes, that was it, she now had a dream, and she smiled just thinking about it.

Savannah looked out at the field where Jonah and John gathered the crops for another year.

Tomorrow there would be much to do, but it excited her to think about all the beautiful, delicious food that would be taken to the underground storage room, to be eaten when the winter set in.

There was talk of another neighbor building their cabin now, not too far from where John's old cabin sat.

Jonah said their names were Noel and Mary Lou Ayers. Savannah could not wait to meet them. Maybe they would all get together with the Ingalls and help them raise their barn.

Savannah grabbed her paper and feather pen, for the words of a new poem had been forming in her head all morning.

> *I left a village, not long ago,*
> *Full of wonder of what would be.*
> *As I worked and prayed, it grew*
> *To get a man's soul free.*
> *And found out what God's love had in store for me,*
> *More love in one man's heart that I thought I deserved.*
> *And as I stand here fulfilled in a man's love,*
> *In his heart well preserved.*
> *A life so full of beauty and wonder,*
> *And just think, One-Hundred, is just a number.*
> *God is so good to me, my heart is so full,*
> *And finding John was no blunder.*
> *Children here, children there, children, children, everywhere!*

Savannah put away her paper and picked up Matthew. "Come on Rose, let's go inside and start dinner for the men; they have worked hard and will be hungry shortly."

Savannah smiled as she started toward the house. Life couldn't get any better than this.

A Letter From Karen

I enjoyed writing *Traded for One Hundred Acres*, because when I was a very small girl, my favorite television shows were those from the old days.

I think perhaps I am an old soul, and as much as I love modern day conveniences, the thought of going back to those days when life was simpler intrigues me.

Trust me, I would not do well in those days, though, because I love electricity, heat with just the control of a switch, cell phones, internet, microwave food, and of course, nice big tubs full of hot water.

As I started writing *Traded for One Hundred Acres*, I only knew I wanted to set a story in that time period and start it in the town of Dahlonega (I love this town) around the time of the first major gold rush.

My daughter, Heather, named the main characters, Savannah and Jonah, and I fell in love with those names, and of course, the characters.

I imagined what it was like for Jonah to have lost the love of his life, and Savannah to come home to find her father had promised her hand in marriage to Jonah, without even speaking to her about it.

Sometimes in life, tragedies happen that cause us to doubt if God exists, as it was with Jonah.

And there are others who have faith so strong that nothing can waver their belief, as it was with Savannah.

And sometimes God places those two together, for the shepherd can lead in the sheep.

Thank goodness, circumstances caused Jonah to once again believe in a loving God who had always been there, even when he felt he was alone. And even though he turned his back on God, God never once turned His back on him.

Isn't this just like life? We find ourselves struggling, and we tend to blame God?

We sometimes question why God is putting us through this and that, and much of the time, we caused it ourselves.

No matter where you find yourself today, or what struggles or problems you are facing, I can assure you that God wants the best for you, and He wants you in good health and to prosper. He wants you to depend on Him for *everything*.

Jesus came to die for your sins, not to condemn them, and He always wants the best for you.

Do you know Jesus as your personal savior?

*****

For God so loved the world that He gave His only begotten Son, That **whosoever** *believeth in Him, should not perish, but have everlasting life.*

John 3:16

****

This has always been my favorite Bible verse, because to me it says it all. The word whosoever means, anyone, everyone, all of us, if we just BELIEVE that Jesus is our Savior.

We can have everlasting life when this life is over. It does not matter what we have done or where we came from. He died for ALL OF US. Isn't that great?

If you have never asked Jesus into your heart and believe that He is the Son of God, God in the flesh, born of the virgin Mary, to live on this earth and die for our sins, and that He rose again after just three days, then humble yourself and ask Him TODAY.

*****

Dear Lord, I believe that You are the Son of God. I believe that You came to this earth to die for my sins. I am asking You today to fill me with Your Holy presence and save my soul. Forgive me, Lord, and save me from past sins. Today, dear Jesus, wipe the slate clean and allow me to start again, a new creation in You.

Thank You, Lord Jesus, for becoming my Savior. Amen.

*****

If you have just prayed the prayer of salvation and asked Jesus to become your Lord and Savior, then I'd like to give you this advice: Make sure if you don't have a Bible, you go and buy one TODAY. The King James Version, or The New Revised Version are both good.

If you cannot afford a Bible, then write to me, and I will mail you one free of charge. I advise you to seek a Bible-believing church and get to know the people there. Learn from them and grow deeper in your relationship with Jesus.

*****

If *Traded for One Hundred Acres* touched your life in any way, I'd love to hear from you. Please email me at: <u>Karenyp46@gmail.com</u> I would love to hear your comments.

*****

You can also find me on Twitter or FaceBook as: Karen Ayers, Author, Motivational Speaker: Click LIKE, and follow along with me daily as I share inspirational quotes and let you know of upcoming books.

*****

For speaking engagements at Churches, Christian schools, Women's Conferences, etc., please allow six to eight weeks' notice.

It would please me to come visit with you and share my own testimony of faith.

*****

Look for other books by Karen Ayers at: www.sbpra.com/KarenAyers

The Secrets of Westingdale
Sweet Summer Rain
Fall's Undying Promise
Cold Winter's Chill
The Fragrance of Spring
Amazing Grace, the Ultimate Forgiveness
Imperfect World, Perfect Me

Review Requested:

If you loved this book, would you please provide a review at Amazon.com?

Lightning Source UK Ltd.
Milton Keynes UK
UKHW041458230719
346677UK00001B/293/P